Mixing business with pleasure...

Luke helped her from the car, pulled her against his body and covered her mouth with his own as he watched the cab retreat down the hill from the corner of his eye.

Jessica stiffened, trying to pull away, but Luke tightened his hold. "Easy, Jess," he murmured over her lips. "A loving couple is the only thing that driver must remember."

She stilled, but he could feel her heartbeat increasing against his chest. To his shock, she opened her mouth tentatively under his.

Heat rocketed through Luke, exciting something savage and hard in him. Before he could stop, knowing full well the taxi had long gone, he deepened his kiss and his tongue met hers. He felt her welcoming him, her body softening against his as she angled her mouth, allowing him to taste her own hot, sweet need.

At the same time his brain was screaming that this was so wrong, for more reasons than he cared to count. She was vulnerable. And she was opening up to him for all the wrong reasons.

Dear Reader,

After setting SHADOW SOLDIERS stories around the globe, I was thrilled to finally bring one to my home turf—a mist-shrouded port city along the Pacific Rim tucked between ocean inlets, dense forests and rugged mountains. A place with a multicultural heritage and a people defined by disparate mores and by the wildness and weather that unites them.

This the backdrop for *The Heart of a Renegade,* the story of an Aussie Shadow Soldier, a born protector who will not be able to save what is most dear to him until he stops protecting himself from love. It takes a woman with real inner strength to breach this bodyguard's armor, but she must do it if they are to defy a deadly enemy.

I hope you enjoy the ride into my end of the Pacific Northwest. For a photo tour of the very real places visited by Luke and Jessica, please visit my Web site at www.lorethannewhite.com.

Loreth Anne White

THE HEART OF A
RENEGADE

Loreth Anne White

Silhouette®
Romantic
SUSPENSE

SILHOUETTE BOOKS

ISBN-13: 978-0-373-27575-5
ISBN-10:   0-373-27575-7

THE HEART OF A RENEGADE

Copyright © 2008 by Loreth Beswetherick

Visit Silhouette Books at www.eHarlequin.com

Printed in U.S.A.

LORETH ANNE WHITE

was born and raised in southern Africa, but now lives in Whistler, a ski resort in the moody British Columbian Coast Mountain range. It's a place of vast, wild and often dangerous mountains, larger-than-life characters, epic adventure and romance—the perfect place to escape reality. It's no wonder it was here she was inspired to abandon a sixteen-year career as a journalist (under the name Loreth Beswetherick) to escape into a world of romantic fiction filled with dangerous men and adventurous women.

When she's not writing, you will find her long-distance running, Nordic walking or skiing the trails and generally trying to avoid the bears—albeit not very successfully. She calls this work, because it's when the best ideas come.

To my editor—Susan Litman,
for continuing to believe in me.

And to Johnny Onefeather, for the brainstorming.

Prologue

Jessica Chan scrambled under the drooping boughs of a giant hemlock, her camera bag dragging through needles and loam, heavy wet branches drenching the thin fabric of her blouse.

Shaking from cold and nerves, she huddled tight against the base of the tree and peered through the curtain of branches as two Asian men emerged from the apartment building across the street.

They stopped, looked down the road for her.

Her heart stalled as she saw the glint of steel in one of the men's hands.

The knife that had just killed her friend Stephanie.

The blade that had been meant for *her*, not her friend.

For a terrifying moment Jessica thought they'd seen her. She shut her eyes, telling herself it was not possible. The winter night was black as pitch, cloud low, freezing rain falling. There were no lights in the park.

One of the men cursed violently in Chinese and her pulse raced.

There was no doubt in Jessica's mind—they were members of the Dragon Heads Triad.

And she was certain they would kill her because of what she'd seen—and photographed—in Chinatown that morning, because of the images still undeveloped on the roll of film in her Minolta camera.

She clutched her camera bag against her chest and watched as the men moved down the street, disappearing into the alley where Stephanie's body lay.

Shivering violently, Jessica remained hidden under the hemlock branches in the park for hours, the image of the men knifing Stephanie rolling in a sickening loop through her brain.

Stephanie Ward had been Jessica's closest friend, her *only* friend in this new city. She had invited Jessica to come to Vancouver from the U.K. to start afresh, offering Jessica a job at the small Canadian television station where she worked.

Jessica had been so grateful. Three years after her brutal kidnapping ordeal in China, she had finally abandoned psychotherapy and drug treatments, and her hallucinations hadn't occurred for a while. She'd thought she was *finally* getting her life back on track.

Until she'd gone shopping in Chinatown that morning.

Until she'd seen—and photographed—Dragon Heads kingpin Xiang-Li, a wanted man in several countries, along with the unnamed man responsible for the pharmacological torture that had nearly destroyed her in China three years ago. A man Jessica called The Chemist.

Those two men had stolen her life. One of them was a man no one would even admit existed.

Jessica had gone straight to cops. She'd told no one else about her photographs apart from the Royal Canadian Mounted Police, but somehow the Triad had still been tipped off.

They'd ransacked her apartment, taken the negatives and prints from the one roll she'd already developed, then come for her. Too afraid to return to the police, Jessica had run to Steph's apartment with the second roll still undeveloped in her camera.

The men must have followed her, been waiting in the dark alley for her to come out. Because of Stephanie's height and coloring they must have mistaken her for Jessica when she'd borrowed Jessica's raincoat and nipped out for cheesecake. They'd realized their mistake when they'd pulled the hood back from Steph's face and looked up to see Jessica standing on the balcony. Watching in horror.

Tears finally filled Jessica's eyes. Steph was dead.

And it was her fault.

It was well after midnight before Jessica finally dared leave the cover of the hemlock. The temperature was plunging and icy needles of rain stung her face. She was shaking uncontrollably, the first stages of hypothermia setting in, confusing her mind.

She had nowhere to go. No one to trust.

Not even the police.

Her cell phone was in the pocket of her coat—on Stephanie's body. So was her driver's license and her keys. The RCMP were going to be looking for her in connection with murder now. And she was being hunted by one of the biggest—and deadliest—Chinese organized crime syndicates.

There was only one person in the world who might be able to help her. Giles Rehnquist, her old colleague in Shanghai, would believe what she'd seen. He'd know what to do. She just had to reach a pay phone and call him in Shanghai.

Before the Triad got to her first.

Chapter 1

Luke Stone hunched over his shopping cart, black wool hat pulled low over his brow, eyes trained on the woman.

A blast of steam roiled from a vent in the sidewalk, disappearing with a white hiss into the frigid February night, but not for one instant did his focus stray from the woman standing alone outside the phone booth.

She was underdressed for these temperatures, shivering as she rubbed bare hands and checked her watch. He noted the heavy camera bag slung over her shoulder.

It was definitely Jessica Chan, ex-BBC foreign correspondent, Shanghai bureau. Here in Gastown at the appointed booth, at the allotted hour. His principal.

Luke no longer accepted close protection gigs. Not since he'd failed to protect the most important people in his life—his wife and unborn child. It was written right into his contract with the Force du Sablé, and he'd refused this job point-blank. But they'd told him he was the only person who could reach Jessica in time. Without Luke's help, she would die.

Tonight.

Luke hoped to be rid of her in a matter of hours. Then he could get back to life the way he liked it. Alone.

The nearby steam clock released a sharp whistle and she jerked round, her straight, waist-length hair shimmering under the neon of the store sign behind her as she spun to face his direction. Her skin was pure porcelain in the eerie light, her exotic eyes glittering. Even from his position he could see they were the color of fine single-malt whiskey. With a small punch to the gut Luke realized the lady was startlingly beautiful. And very, very frightened.

She had reason to be.

Not only were the cops after her, she was being hunted by one of deadliest Asian gangs in existence. Now the CIA wanted her, too—ever since she'd placed a call to undercover CIA operative Giles Rehnquist based at the CNN bureau in Shanghai two days ago.

That phone call had cost Rehnquist his life.

And that's why Luke was here now, to bring her in and to hand her—and the film in her camera—over to the CIA before she died, too.

She didn't know yet that her "journalist" friend would not be there to take the call she was about to place. To the best of Luke's knowledge, Jessica Chan had no idea Rehnquist was CIA.

It was almost 11:00 p.m. now, the time Rehnquist had told her to phone him from this booth, and a dank fog was crawling up from the docks, fingering through the historic brick alleys that led off in all directions.

Luke tossed a can into his cart as he inched closer. The sound caught her attention and she shot a look directly at him, missing what had just snared *his* interest—an Asian man in a leather jacket lingering just beyond a pool of light that spilled from a restaurant window.

The Asian quietly signaled another man in a dark doorway down the street. Both were watching Jessica, closing in on her from either end of the alley.

Luke pushed his cart faster toward his principal, head bent low as he mumbled to himself.

The Gastown steam clock shot out a powerful blast and began the hourly Windsor chimes. It was eleven o'clock. Jessica Chan stepped into the booth, picked up the receiver and rapidly began to punch in numbers.

A car drove by, tires crackling on slick cobblestones as tiny flakes of snow began to crystallize in the frigid air. By the time the vehicle had passed, Luke had lost visuals on both men.

His pulse quickened and he unholstered his weapon.

Giles was *dead?*

Jessica clenched the phone, her mouth turning dry as she tried to absorb what the woman at the CNN bureau in Shanghai was telling her. The one man who could help her was…gone. Confusion clouded her brain.

She'd spoken to him only two days ago, after Stephanie's murder. She'd told him everything.

Giles had instructed her to lay low in a cheap hotel, use only cash and call him back from this exact same pay phone in forty-eight hours. In the meantime he'd find a way to help her. He had been Jessica's last resort.

Her *only* hope.

And now he was dead.

Panic strafed her chest as the implications hit her and she slammed down the receiver. But just as she turned to run, a gunshot shattered a pane of glass near her ear.

She screamed and dropped down, covering her head with both hands and scrunching her eyes tight as a hail of bullets blew out another pane and shards rained down over her.

There was a moment of deathly silence before another exchange of gunfire shattered a store window across the street. Jessica heard glass tinkle to the frozen sidewalk. A security alarm began to wail. A woman screamed. More shouts came from the opposite direction as footsteps rang out on the cobblestones and a man yelled for someone to call 911.

She had to leave before the cops arrived.

Clutching her camera bag, Jessica surged to her feet, but as she tried to bolt from the booth, a man grabbed her, yanking her forcibly backward. Jessica screamed, fighting back with every ounce of strength. But she was no match against his iron grip. He whirled her round to face him and her heart clean stopped.

It was the Dumpster diver, morphed from a bent and fragile shape into something huge, ominous and incredibly powerful. He reeked of old booze, yet his pale gray eyes were sharp as flint against his grease-blackened face.

She opened her mouth in terror, but he pressed a gloved palm over it. "Don't make a sound," he whispered against her ear. "I'm here to help you."

He released her mouth slowly, testing her resolve. But Jessica couldn't have uttered a word if she'd tried.

She couldn't even breathe.

He took her jaw in powerful fingers, twisting her face quickly toward the light. "Looks okay," he said, wiping blood from her cheek with a callused thumb. "Just a shallow cut." His voice was rough gravel, his accent Australian.

Out of the corner of her eye Jessica could see a man's body splayed inhumanly across the sidewalk, a gun at his side. Another body sprawled to the right of him. Both were Asian. People were gathering around them.

Her eyes shot back to the man holding her. He was holstering a pistol. *He'd* shot those men. He'd just saved her from the triad. She struggled to absorb the contradicting images he telegraphed. His tattered gloves had no fingertips, his hat was old black wool, his jacket threadbare tweed. He stunk of booze, yet there was no alcohol on his breath. She couldn't make any sense of him.

The yelling and footsteps grew louder, and police sirens began to wail.

Jessica shot a last desperate look down the road, toward the sound of approaching sirens. Right now she didn't know which was the worse evil—the police who'd betrayed her, or him.

"You don't want the cops, Jessica," he warned, his fingers encircling her arm.

He knew her name! Her eyes whipped back to him.

He drew her body firmly up against his. "Listen to me, Jessica," he said quietly. "I can tell you what happened to Giles Rehnquist, but right now your life depends on following my orders. Now *run.*"

He hunkered low, pulling her by the hand at a clip over irregular paving as the sirens grew louder. They ducked into Blood Alley, and he forced her hard up against a rough brick wall as Vancouver Police Department cruisers converged on the scene of the shooting, car doors swinging open, officers barking commands. Cops quickly began to fan out, heading their way with flashlights beaming through the fog.

"This way," he whispered, pulling her after him. They ran for the alley exit, but a squad car slowed in front of it, barring their escape. He turned and shoved her down between two overflowing Dumpsters that flanked the service entrance of an Irish pub, pinning her down firmly against bags of garbage with his weight. "Don't move," he murmured against her hair. The smothering stench of stale sweat and booze permeating the tattered tweed of his jacket made her gag, but the soft sweater against his hard body smelled soapy clean. Masculine.

Jessica closed her eyes, trying to calm herself. She could feel the strong, steady beat of his heart against her chest. It was a strangely comforting sensation. In a foreign city where she'd been cut off from everything including her clothes, apartment, cell phone and colleagues—a city where she was beginning to wonder if she could even trust her own mind—this man felt solid. He felt real. Capable. And he hadn't betrayed her.

Yet.

The sounds in the distance grew less frenetic, but still her rescuer didn't move and her legs were going numb. She tried to wiggle feeling back into her toes.

"Keep still," he hissed. "Someone's coming."

Then she heard it: the steady *clop, clop, clop,* of hooves on cobblestones. She peered out from under his jacket as the silhouettes of two police officers on horses darkened the entrance to Blood Alley, fog swirling behind them.

The mounted police entered the alley slowly, hooves echoing as they panned darkened crevices with flashlights.

Jessica's throat tightened, but the steady beat of her defender's heart never faltered. Not even when the hooves drew so near they almost touched his feet. One of the horses snorted, hot breath steaming into the air. She could smell them.

"Hey, you," one of the cops said, directing his flashlight into their corner. "Can you get to your feet, please? I need to see ID."

The man lying on top of Jessica groaned, made as if he was trying to sit up, then he flopped back as if too drunk.

The officer dismounted. "Can you stand, buddy?" the cop said, reaching down to pull him up. Her mysterious savior waited until the cop's center of balance was precisely at the most disadvantageous, then he grabbed the policeman's arm, yanked him down, cracked his head against his own, and rolled out from under him as the unconscious cop slumped heavily onto Jessica. She stifled a yelp of shock.

The officer on his horse immediately drew his weapon, yelling at him to freeze, but her protector surged forward with such swift and fluid motion it caught the officer by surprise. He fired, his bullet going wild and pinging into the Dumpster over Jessica's head as her defender grabbed the cop with bare hands and dragged him from his horse.

The horse reared, hooves clawing at air before taking off with a clatter over stone. Jessica stared in awe as her guardian rendered the policeman unconscious with quick, firm pressure of his hand to the man's neck.

She'd seen people trained in martial arts do that. She'd seen them move like him, too—fast and powerful, balletic. This man was skilled in hand-to-hand combat. He was a walking, talking lethal weapon.

Fear squeezed at her heart.

He dragged the unconscious V.P.D. officer off her and checked his pulse, before rolling the man gently onto the garbage bags and positioning his head so he could breathe easily.

He held his hand out to Jessica. "Come."

"What…what about the policemen?"

"They'll wake in a few minutes. We've got to move. Fast."

She stared up at him, the beam from the fallen flashlight catching the icy glint in his eerily pale eyes. He wasn't even breathing hard. Jessica shrank back into the garbage, suddenly terrified, the aftereffects of adrenaline combined with the cold, making her shake violently.

"You want to live, don't you?" he said.

She nodded. He reached down, grabbed her wrist and jerked her firmly to her feet. "Come, then."

He guided her through a twisting network of narrow black alleys that stunk of urine and decay, moving in the direction of the water.

They crossed the railway tracks into a deserted dockyard. The fog was thicker down by the sea, inky water slapping softly against old wood pylons, the scent of brine heavy.

"Quietly," he whispered, taking her hand as they slipped between two massive rows of shipping containers. He held her back against ice-cold steel, waiting until he was certain they hadn't been followed.

Jessica's breathing was ragged, her lungs burning from running in the cold, her pulse pounding wildly. But beside her, his body was as calm and still as a practiced and patient predator. She had no doubt this man could kill with his bare hands and without compunction.

"Who are you—?"

He clapped his hand suddenly over her mouth, and pointed. Another cop car cruised quietly across the harbor entrance, flashing lights creating pulsing halos of white, red and blue in the dense fog.

He removed his hand as the cruiser moved on. "Sorry," he whispered. "Come—"

But Jessica didn't move. She felt suddenly paralyzed with exhaustion and she couldn't seem to order her thoughts.

He tilted her chin and looked into her eyes. "You okay?"

"Please…just tell me who you are," she whispered.

"My name's Luke Stone. You ready to run again?" He didn't wait for an answer. He grasped her wrist and dragged her in a crouching sprint across the empty parking lot toward the black water.

They stopped at a dock pylon, Jessica panting hard. Between them and the North Shore lay nothing but the frigid expanse of the Burrard Inlet. Snowflakes began to swirl bigger and softer, disappearing into the black void below her feet.

He edged her toward the dock edge. "You first. Down there."

"What?"

He swore softly and grabbed her hands, drawing her into a crouch. He placed both her hands on a frozen metal rung. "Hang on to this. Put your leg over the side, feel for the next rung with your foot, climb all the way down to the inflatable. One step at a time."

Panic whipped through her. "I…I don't see any inflatable."

"It's down there, in the dark. Trust me."

Her eyes shot to his. She didn't trust *anyone*.

"Jess," his eyes held hers steadily. "They killed your friend because of what you saw in Chinatown. They killed Giles because you told him. Believe me, they *will* kill you, too. Don't give them that chance, okay?" He touched her cheek gently. "I'm here to help you."

Emotion exploded through her chest and she tightened her grip on the rung.

This man simply accepted what the cops hadn't—that she really *had* seen those men, that her life *was* in danger. *He believed her.* Surely that placed him somewhere on her side?

"You got the film in that bag?"

She said nothing.

"Give it to me, Jess."

"I…I'd rather hold on to it."

He swore again. "Look, we don't have time for this. Give me your bag." He reached to take it.

But she pulled back, overbalancing as she did, her foot shooting out from under her, lurching her down toward the ocean. He grabbed her, halting a certain plunge into the icy water. His fingers dug into her arm as she swayed out over the water. "If want my help, Jessica, you give me that bag and you get down into that boat. Fast. Understand?"

There was something in his voice that warned her not to cross him.

Her throat turned dry and her eyes watered as she let him take the one thing from her that could prove her sanity and buy back her credibility—proof that the man who'd tortured her in China three years ago was real.

"Thank you. Now go."

Heart slamming against her ribs, she swung her leg out, searching for purchase on the old ladder, and she descended blindly into the darkness.

Luke cursed to himself, willing her to speed it up as he scanned the shadowed dockyard, weapon in hand, her camera bag slung across his chest.

This was supposed to have been a simple in-and-out job—pick up the principal at the pay phone, take her back to his place, call it in, arrange to ship her out. It sure as hell hadn't panned out that way.

Somehow the Dragon Heads—if that's who those two men were—had gotten wind she'd be at that pay phone. And they'd ambushed her.

He'd just killed two of their members. Those guys tended to hold grudges. He'd also assaulted a couple of V.P.D. cops. There was going to be a fair grudge there, too.

Damn it to hell. Jessica Chan had just sucked him right into her shadowy mess, all the way up to the bloody hilt. The triad, the RCMP and the city police were all going to be out for his blood now, too.

"Way to go, Stone," he muttered to himself. *So much for keeping a low profile. At least you got the girl.*

Trouble was, he didn't want the girl.

He didn't want to be responsible for protecting another woman. Ever. If he failed again, it would kill him.

Inky ripples fanned out in the ocean as she stepped into the Zodiac. "I'm in," Jessica whispered from below. And for one insane and fleeting second, Luke almost thought about leaving her. Right there. On her own. In the boat.

Because she scared him.

It wasn't her beauty or the fact she smelled and felt too damn good when pressed against him. She was frightened. Vulnerable. And she needed him.

Luke didn't want to be needed.

He didn't want to care about anyone.

But being close to Jessica Chan had awakened something dangerous inside him. Something better off left dormant, preferably dead.

But the beast inside him had stirred. And Luke Stone knew instinctively that he was in trouble.

Chapter 2

Luke steered the inflatable into the choppy shipping lanes of Burrard Inlet. They had no lights and their small craft was dangerously invisible to bigger ships.

Jessica drew the black plastic sheet Luke had placed over her shoulders tightly around her neck in an attempt to shut out the insidious cold. "Wh-what happened to Giles?" She was shivering so badly she was stuttering.

"Shh, not now," he whispered. "Sound carries over the water."

A tanker loomed suddenly out of the mist and a foghorn blared. A monster hull sliced through the darkness in front of them, causing a surge of waves that broadsided their little boat, sending them bobbing like a cork.

But Luke held the Zodiac steady as he calmly negotiated the churning white water of the big ship's wake. Nothing seemed to knock this man's steely control.

As they neared the North Shore the sea turned glassy and the air grew quiet. All Jessica could hear as they neared the lights of Lonsdale Quay was the low drone of their small engine and the soft slap of water under their hull. It was around midnight, no movement on the pier, the Lonsdale market long closed.

Luke guided their craft past a row of tugboats as he maneuvered into a small working harbor and bumped up against a dock. He tossed out a rope, secured the craft and reached for her hand. "Leave the plastic in the boat," he whispered.

"It's freezing," she protested.

"You can have my jacket."

"It stinks."

He laughed softly. "I don't mean this one," he said as he shrugged out of the booze-drenched tweed. He reached under the dock, fiddled with some knots and rope, pulled a garbage bag free and opened it. "This one," he said, withdrawing a black leather jacket and draping it over her shoulders.

He removed his tattered gloves, palmed the wool hat off his head and ruffled his hair before dropping to his haunches and floating the old jacket out into the dockyard water along with the hat and gloves. Bemused, Jessica watched as he dipped a handkerchief into the sea and wiped the black camouflage grease from his face. He stuffed the handkerchief back into his pant pocket, stood to his full height, and slung her camera bag across his massive chest.

There was enough light coming from the SeaBus terminal for Jessica to see his hair was sandy blond, short and rumpled. His features craggy, strong, and tanned against his startlingly pale gray eyes. He was now clad in black jeans, black boots and a black turtleneck sweater which emphasized the breadth of his shoulders and the muscle in his arms. Not the slightest hint of the broken homeless character she'd seen shuffling behind the shopping cart lingered in his physique.

A chameleon, she thought. One who shifted shape at will. And he'd clearly planned every step of their escape. A cool whisper of warning ruffled through her and with it came the renewed bite of fear.

He checked his watch, and hooked his arm casually through hers. "You're my date, okay? Let's go."

"I'm…what?"

"The last SeaBus is coming over from the city now. We're going to blend with the commuters as they disembark and drift toward the car park and bus loop. Then we're going to walk up to a nightclub on Esplanade, grab a hot dog at the late-night stand outside the club and I'm going to hail a cab to take us to a false address. No talking in the cab, not one word, understand?"

"Luke, please—" she tried to draw him to a halt. "I need to know what happened to—"

"Later. All the cab driver must recall is an ordinary couple coming out of the club. Nothing else, got it?"

She pulled her arm free. "No," she whispered angrily. "I don't get it. There is *nothing* ordinary about us. I have *no* idea who you are or where you're taking me. Do you think I'm nuts? You think I'm just going to along with—" she wagged her hand at him "—whatever some lethal cross between James Bond and Crocodile Dundee orders me to do? You just assaulted two cops back there. You *killed* two men. I—"

He seized her arm, pulled her close, his eyes narrowing to sharp steel slivers. "Dammit, Jessica, keep it down. I saved your life back there."

"And I'm grateful. But I don't trust *anyone*, especially foreign men with guns who want what's in my camera."

He studied her in silence for a long beat. "I know why you don't trust anyone," he said quietly. "It's because no one trusts you." He tilted her chin up. "Not since your abduction and torture in China. Am I right?"

She swallowed a ballooning hurt in her throat.

Luke was right. The incident had cost her everything, most importantly her career, her pride and her hard-won respect. As the unacknowledged, illegitimate daughter of a British diplomat and his Chinese mistress Jessica had felt driven all her life to prove her worth in this world, to dig herself out of her impoverished London background. To make something of herself.

She'd done it for her mother.

She'd done it to show she didn't need the acknowledgment

or support of her wealthy father. She'd done it for her own sense of self-worth, and she'd succeeded. She'd become a rising star with the BBC, one of their top foreign correspondents. There was even talk of hosting her own news show.

But it had all vanished three years ago, the day she'd been kidnapped from Shanghai's business district and taken to a remote factory warehouse in Hubei province where members of the Dragon Heads and an official from the Chinese government had accused her of being a spy for the United States.

She'd been tortured for information and injected with mind-altering hallucinogenic "truth drugs," designed and administered by the man she called The Chemist. A man she believed was a top level biochemical assassin for a covert arm of the ruling Chinese Communist Party which was using the Dragon Heads to further its political agenda worldwide.

Jessica had managed a harrowing escape, but the drugs had permanently damaged her brain, leaving her with horrific flashbacks and hallucinations. The hallucinations were so real that she could no longer be certain of her ability to discern reality from fiction. The Chinese government denied any involvement and she had no proof of a government cover-up. In the end, she'd been swept under the bureaucratic carpet. She'd lost her job, and she'd been left to languish in a British mental institution with severe depression, paranoia, hallucinations, labeled a schizophrenic.

But Jessica had fought back.

She knew what she'd endured in China was true, even if her own memories of the ordeal were sketchy. And now she finally had some proof. The film in her camera was going to show The Chemist really did exist and that he was here, right now, in North America, with Dragon Heads boss Xiang-Li.

"Not even the RCMP took your word that what you just saw in Chinatown wasn't another of your well-documented hallucinations. That's why they told you to come back with the prints, once you'd developed them. Am I right, Jess?"

She looked away.

But Luke drew her firmly against his torso as a bus passed on the road above them. His body was so incredibly solid, so warm. Big. He felt so confoundingly safe and dangerous at the same time.

A terrified and very lonely part of Jessica ached to lean into him, to have him hold her, have *anyone* hold her. To have someone care.

"Let me tell you something, Jess," he said quietly. "I believe you. Those guys shooting at you in Gastown were real. That tells me that what you saw in Chinatown was real, too. And someone is prepared to kill to keep it quiet. They want the evidence in your camera and they want you dead. And now they want me, too." He paused, watching her face intently. "That puts you and me pretty much on the same side, wouldn't you say?"

She closed her eyes. The idea of an ally, someone who actually believed she wasn't a total nut job, was so heady and alluring it hurt. After being alone and confused for so many years she'd come to a point where she'd actually believed she *was* crazy, where she honestly didn't know whether she could trust her own mind. The doubt still whispered, even now.

Tears burned under her lids as she struggled to hold back the painful surge of emotion. "Why are you doing this for me, Luke?"

The question punched at him in a way Luke couldn't explain. This woman got to him. He'd seen her file. He knew her background. He knew what she'd endured and he understood her kind of solitude. And while she was afraid and vulnerable, she was also brave. Never mind utterly physically compelling.

He exhaled heavily.

He didn't want anything to get to him. He didn't want to understand her. Hell, he didn't even want to *like* her.

He didn't want to like *anybody*.

"I'm not doing it for you, Jess." His voice was suddenly blunt and he knew it but couldn't help it. "It's my job. I work for the Force du Sablé, a private military company that offers close protection to politically sensitive targets, among other things." He paused, angry again that this mission had been thrust on him by FDS boss Jacques Sauvage.

"Politically sensitive targets?" she whispered.

"The FDS was contracted by the CIA to find you and to bring you in. I'm your bodyguard until I hand you and the film over." Which he hoped to hell would happen within the next few hours.

Panic sparked in her eyes. "How does the CIA know about my film? How do *you* know about it? How do you even know about Giles?"

"Later, Jess. Right now I need to get you someplace you can sleep for the night." He took her arm and guided her up the narrow gangplank. He'd wasted enough time. It wasn't his job to explain anything. This mission had come on such short notice Luke wasn't the hell sure what he *could* tell her.

The only reason he was on this dock right now was because Jacques Sauvage had informed him that Jessica Chan would die tonight without his immediate intervention.

The FDS had stationed Luke in Vancouver to gather intelligence on Asian organized crime syndicates that operated out of the Pacific Northwest, particularly gangs rumored to be colluding with known terrorist organizations—like the Dragon Heads.

The FDS was finding increased client demand for this sort of intelligence and Luke's brief had been to establish a small intelligence office in the city.

This had positioned him as the only operative the FDS could dispatch to Jessica in time. In *spite* of his contract.

Now he was saddled with a job he could neither refuse nor fully embrace. He cursed silently. Jacques was going to pay for this.

"Where?" she asked.

"Where what?"

"You said you were going to take me someplace I could sleep for the night."

"Right. I guess that would be…my place." Luke swore to himself again.

Yeah, Jacques was going to pay big-time, *especially* if he didn't get this woman off his hands within the next few hours.

* * *

The cab was warm and it relaxed his principal—which was how Luke was determined to think of Jessica Chan from this point on. He put his arm around her in an effort to appear a casual couple, while he clamped down on his emotions. She was exhausted and within minutes she'd fallen asleep nestled right into the crook of his arm. Reluctantly he realized she fit perfectly.

Too perfectly.

She felt too damn good.

Old protective instincts began to rustle uncomfortably. Being a bodyguard had come as naturally to him as beating up the bully who'd picked on the smaller kids in the schoolyard. And it had brought him just as much trouble.

Luke had simply been born to protect, especially when he perceived injustice. But for the last four years, he'd managed to hold those instincts at bay, for his own survival. Now, holding Jessica in his arms, he could feel the echo whispering through him again, pulsing louder and stronger with every beat of his heart. Luke swallowed against the sudden dryness in his throat.

The taxi bumped over a speed hump and the soft weight of Jessica's—*his principal's*—breast pressed into his chest, awakening something in quite another part of Luke's body.

He closed his eyes, grudgingly unable to stop savoring the sweet sexual sensation stirring low in his gut. Luke realized with mild shock that he didn't actually want to block it out. It felt good to have a woman in his arms again, to feel his blood and body roused again. His pulse quickened and his throat turned even drier.

The cab pulled up in front of the West Vancouver address Luke had given the driver, and not a moment too soon. "Wake up," he said, gently nudging her.

Her almond-shaped eyes fluttered open, sultry with sleep, then widened in shock at the sudden realization of where she was.

"It's okay, we're here."

Luke settled the fare, helped her from the car and, without a word, pulled her against his body and covered her mouth with his own as he watched the red brake lights of the cab retreat down the hill from the corner of his eye.

Jessica stiffened, trying to pull away, but Luke tightened his hold. "Easy, Jess," he murmured over her lips as he watched the taxi round a corner. "A loving couple is the only thing that driver must remember."

She stilled in his arms, but he could feel her heartbeat increasing rapidly against his chest. To his shock, she opened her mouth tentatively under his.

Heat rocketed through Luke, exciting something savage and hard in him. Before he could stop, knowing full well the taxi had long gone, he deepened his kiss and his tongue met hers. He felt her welcoming him, her body softening against his as she angled her mouth, allowing him to taste her own hot, sweet need.

Luke couldn't breathe. He closed his eyes, allowing his iron grip on control to ease for the first time in years, simply giving himself over to sensation, tasting her deep, hungrily, not bothering to fight the mounting pressure of his arousal against her belly, which he knew she had to feel.

At the same time his brain was screaming that this was so wrong, for more reasons than he cared to count. She was his principal. And vulnerable. And she was opening to him for all the wrong reasons.

Luke managed to pull back, breathing hard. They locked gazes for a moment, words defying them. And he could see just as much dark turbulence and confusion in those exquisite amber eyes of hers as he felt in his heart.

He wanted to explain why he'd done this. But he didn't know the answer himself.

Instead he cleared his throat and said, "We should go."

She simply nodded.

Luke escorted her to his innocuous dark blue SUV parked along the curb, taking exaggerated care not to touch her again as he beeped the alarm, opened the passenger door and let her in.

But letting Jessica Chan in was the last thing in this world Luke was ready to do.

He had a sinking feeling the more he opened the door to this woman, the harder it would become to get her back out of his life.

Tasting her had been intoxicating, like the first heady sip of elixir for an alcoholic. Just as addictive and potentially just as lethal to him.

Hot damn, he was in trouble. Serious trouble.

Luke slammed the door shut and wiped his mouth roughly with the back of his hand. Jacques better have that pickup ready because he wanted to be rid of this woman before sunrise.

Luke drove over the Lions Gate Bridge, back toward the heart of downtown Vancouver, car heater cranked high, soft classical music playing, snowflakes swirling at them like asteroids in the headlights. For the first time in days Jessica felt safe—on one level.

But on another, she wasn't so sure.

She studied him surreptitiously as orange-hued streetlights pulsed over his rugged profile, throwing a small scar that fanned from the corner of his right eye into relief.

He had another fine scar across his chin and another that ran down his neck.

He looked ruggedly handsome, scarred, dangerous.

"Are you going to tell me about Giles now?" she asked.

He hesitated. "I need to check in with my people before I can explain. This was…sort of a rush job," he said, turning off the bridge and heading toward Granville Island, where he pulled into a parking lot near the marina and killed the engine.

"You sound pissed to be saddled with me. Are you?"

He wouldn't look at her.

"Why don't you just say it like it is, Luke? It's not like I haven't endured worse."

His eyes flashed to hers, a hint of guilt in them. "It's nothing personal," he said flatly. "I'd moved out of the close-protection business."

"Why?"

"Not my thing."

"Great," she muttered to herself. A reluctant bodyguard. She'd almost made the mistake of thinking he cared. Just a little. A part of her actually *wanted* him to care. The loneliness in Jess wanted to attach meaning to his incredible soul-searing kiss.

A dark sense of depression descended on her. She was a fool to be so needy. It made her angry.

He got out, came round to the passenger side, her camera bag in his hand, and he opened the door. "Coming?"

She closed her eyes for a moment and sucked in a deep breath of cold ocean air mixed with brine. "Yeah. I guess I'm flat out of choices."

He jutted his chin toward a row of houseboats interspersed with yachts. "My place is down there, on the water."

The snow was dumping heavily now, big fat flakes waltzing on the wind and shimmying in the halos of lights that lined the wooden boardwalk to the boathouses. It was settling fast on the yachts and the stacked rows of kayaks, but the flakes melted into blackness as they hit the glistening dark water of False Creek.

He took her arm. "Careful. The boardwalk gets slippery."

A quiver of heat shot through Jessica as her body connected with his again. She cursed to herself, wondering if his attentiveness was chivalry or chauvinism.

Or just another aspect of a job he didn't want.

Chapter 3

Luke strode into his living room, booted up his laptop and set his satellite phone next to it. He hooked his finger into the hem of his sweater and pulled it up over his head as he walked to the bathroom, desperate to scrub the lingering scent of booze from his skin and from his memory, knowing at the same time no matter how hard he abraded himself, he was never going to scrape deep enough to eradicate the drunken nightmares that lingered in the dark crevices of his brain.

"I'm going to take a shower," he called back to her as he went around the corner, leaving her standing alone in the middle of his living room. He'd check in with Jacques as soon as he was done. "Make yourself at home. Take anything you want from the kitchen."

"I might just leave!" she yelled after him, irritation snipping her voice suddenly.

He stilled, turned and stepped shirtless back around the corner, his eyes narrowing onto her. "Jess, all that stands between you and a bullet right now is me. I think you're smart enough to see that." He turned to go, hesitated, spun back. "But if you really want to go, please, be my guest."

"You said it was your job to protect me," she called out.

"Never wanted the damn job in the first place," he muttered to himself as he kept on walking. He stepped into the bathroom, shut the door and turned the shower on scalding hot. Jacques and the FDS crew could wait. She'd be safe here. Neither the Triad nor the cops had a handle on his identity.

And he was damn sure she wasn't going to leave. Jessica Chan's memories might be pharmacologically cross-wired, but he doubted the rest of her brain was. The lady knew how to survive. She'd made it two days on her own with Chinese assassins after her blood. And he was impressed with how she handled tonight.

She *wanted* to survive.

He had to respect that. Luke knew just how easy it was to give up.

Jessica stared openmouthed at the space Luke Stone had just vacated. The man had one of the most ripped bodies she'd ever had the pleasure of personally encountering. But it was the back he'd turned on her that truly shocked.

Every little bit of exposed skin was crisscrossed with long, pale scars, as though he'd been lashed and shredded within mere inches of his life.

She began to tremble. She steadied herself by reaching out for the back of his couch.

Luke Stone understood torture.

Maybe…just maybe…this man would understand her.

She heard the shower go on and she ran her hands over her hair trying to force rational thought. Panic could bring the hallucinations on again, the doctors had told her that. She had to focus on the present. On moving forward. It was her *only* option. If she lost her grasp on reality now, they'd finally win.

She was never going to let them win.

She realized she still had Luke's leather jacket on though it was warm in his home. He'd put on the gas fire and the kettle on his way through the kitchen.

She slipped out of his jacket, draped it over the couch and went to the floor-to-ceiling windows of his small living room. The windows looked right onto the water. He had a kayak tethered to a small deck and a bike was chained against the wall. The lights of English Bay twinkled on the opposite side of False Creek, everything muted by softly falling snow. It was a pretty place. She wondered if the yacht she'd seen moored to the side of the double-story boathouse was also his. She suspected it was.

She turned to take in the rest of his living space. It was paneled wood and purely male—the home of an outdoorsman. Touring skis and a snowboard hung from racks near the door. Technical snowshoes were propped against the wall near a hall closet that hung slightly ajar, exposing a tangle of ropes, carabiners and jackets.

Contour maps, a compass and a GPS device cluttered his dining table. Jessica walked over and examined the maps. They were of British Columbia's backcountry. Luke Stone's physique was honed by an obvious passion for the wilderness. He had a taste for thrill, adventure. She glanced up at the framed black-and-white photographs that covered one wall. Their evocative beauty drew her closer.

With mild shock, Jessica realized he'd taken them. He'd signed them in the bottom right corners. A shimmer of interest rippled through her as she peered closely at the haunting images. She understood photography—the artistic nuances of black-and-white in particular.

Black-and-white film was what she used. It was her sanity and she clung to it even in a digital era. Two years ago a nurse Jessica had befriended while in the psychiatric institution in England had given her an old Minolta camera. Jessica started using it to record her days, proving to herself that her day-to-day life was real, not imagined, that her memories of it were true. She'd become good at it. And when she'd started developing her own work, the act of watching those daily memories take literal shape in the darkroom had filled Jessica's heart with indescribable joy. With progressive skill in the darkroom came increased mental confidence. That old Minolta had given Jessica the strength to fight back, the will to believe in herself.

Taking photographs had saved her.

Now it looked as though it might destroy her.

She leaned forward and closely examined Luke's images. The way he captured light and contrasting shadow was beautiful. Poignant. He'd shot mountain peaks and ragged cliffs. Eagles, a grizzly. Oceans and ice at sunset. Deserts with nothing but undulating dunes for miles. A wolf pup in snow. A cougar in the crook of two branches. But no humans. Not even a footprint.

She touched a framed image of a small bear cub watching its mother. The look of need and dependence in the young animal's eyes filled Jessica's chest with aching emotion. It was poetic. All the images were. They told her that whoever had held this camera and captured these wild scenes had soul. It was an almost elegiac vision of life in its raw, harsh beauty. Luke Stone had a beautiful mind buried somewhere in that rugged brawn and Jessica suspected there was something sad in there, too.

Because there was sadness in these pictures.

She wondered if he was always alone when he shot his film. Did he need these open spaces for his sanity? Was this his freedom? She had a sense the man was a true loner, a transient who didn't put down roots easily. Perhaps that's why he lived here on the water—it offered a sense of escape.

She heard the shower go off and a voyeuristic guilt pinged through her. She turned quickly to take in the rest of the room before he returned. There was no sign of family or girlfriends— no female touch in the decor at all. The only sign of human connection was a small color print pinned to his fridge with a magnet. It showed three rugged and weather-browned men on pack horses in a red desert. She couldn't make out the faces, but she thought one might be Luke.

Jessica's eyes settled on his computer.

She glanced in the direction of the bathroom. What did she have to lose?

She hastened over to it, quickly tapped a key that brought the monitor to life, saw a file with her name. Her pulse quickened.

She shot another look over her shoulder and clicked on the file. Her breath caught in her throat. Her life, everything, it was all there.

She scrolled rapidly through the information, her body going hot. He had photographs, her résumé, stories on her abduction in China, the name of her mental institution in the U.K., her psychiatrist's notes, the medication she was on, even a virtual transcript of her conversation with Giles two days ago...she heard the bathroom door open. Her breath lodged in her throat.

She quickly closed the file and moved to the opposite end of the room, heart beating fast. She hugged herself, feeling violated in a way she couldn't even begin to articulate.

Why *shouldn't* he have a dossier on her, if he'd been sent to find her? But why was the CIA suddenly interested in her when everyone else had hung her out to dry in China?

She began to feel small again. Afraid. And that horribly familiar panic began to nip at her brain.

"Hey?"

She jumped, whipped her eyes to him.

He stood drying his hair with a towel, wearing a white T-shirt and jeans faded in places she shouldn't look. God, he was good-looking. In a rough and untamed way. He seemed too tough to have the sensitivity for those photographs. Yet there was something in the desolate gray of his eyes, the way the lines fanned softly out from them, that echoed the haunting vistas in the photos.

"You okay?" he said, stilling the towel as he studied her face.

"Yeah, I—I'm fine. Did...you take all of those?" she pointed to the wall.

"Yep."

"They're beautiful."

"Thanks. You want to take a shower? Water's hot." He smiled

and it reached into those wilderness eyes, giving her a thump of sensation in her stomach.

"I…" she became cognizant of the fact she probably stank of garbage and old liquor from that jacket he'd worn. "I guess I should, huh?"

He nodded. "Yep."

"I don't have any clean clothes," she hesitated. "I guess I'm stating the obvious." She felt awkward. Seeing those photographs made her feel as though she'd somehow seen him naked. It was a language she spoke, and when you came across someone who communicated in the same visceral way you did, the link was there whether you wanted it or not.

"I left some stuff for you in the bathroom," he said. "It was the best I could do for now. We can pick up some things for you later. Coffee or tea?"

"I…coffee would be great, thanks."

"Bathroom's that way, down the hall."

She began to walk, stopped. "You're really casual about this," she said. "You say it's not your thing, but…you've done it a lot, haven't you?"

"Picked up women and brought them home? Yeah, I do that a lot." He said it with such a deadpan expression in his flat Australian tone she wasn't sure whether he was joking or not.

"I mean…never mind." She began to make her way to the bathroom.

"You mean killing a couple of gangsters, assaulting two cops and then coming home to make coffee?"

She stopped. "Yes, something like that."

He tossed his towel over a chair at the table, opened a cupboard and took two mugs out. "Your accent is cute, you know that?" he said, plunking the mugs on the counter.

"And you know exactly what part of the U.K. it comes from, too. It's all in that dossier on your computer, so please don't play games with me, Stone."

His eyes flicked between her and his computer and his features turned serious. He stood to his full height, facing her squarely. There was a latent aggression in his posture that made her nervous.

"You looked at my laptop?"

"I'd like to know what is going on and what happened to Giles in Shanghai."

His eyes narrowed slowly. Then a ghost of a smile played at the corners of his strong mouth. "Fair enough," he said, and he turned and reached for a box of green tea. "Take your shower and we'll sit down and talk."

Luke felt her eyes boring into his back. He ignored her as he poured boiling water over a tea bag.

He'd underestimated Jessica. He'd do well to remember she was once an aggressive and respected investigative journalist. Landing a gig as a foreign correspondent for the BBC needed a fair degree of global savvy.

He heard her leave the room, then heard the bathroom door bang shut.

He extracted the tea bag, squeezed it as he listened for the shower. She'd be busy for a few minutes. He positioned himself in front of his laptop, set his mug of tea down and punched Jacques Sauvage's number into his satellite phone. Luke checked his watch as it rang. Dawn would be breaking soon.

"Stone, it's about bloody time. Have you secured the principal?"

"Good morning to you, too, Sauvage. I have her. But we have a complication." He proceeded to tell Jacques about his altercation with the police and the two gangsters.

Jacques was silent for a moment. "This is going to make any sort of cooperation with local law enforcement close to impossible."

Luke shrugged, sipped his tea. "I made an executive decision. Those guys were out to kill her. My guess is they're Dragon Heads, affiliated with Xiang-Li. They don't want the photos getting out."

"You manage to drop the tail?"

"Yep." He sipped from his mug. "What can I tell her?"

"Everything. I'm liaising personally with CIA director Blake Weston on this and he's given no instructions to hold anything back from her. All he wants is the woman, her film and her testimony. He's setting up some form of witness protection for her."

"When are you sending someone to pick her up?"

Jacques hesitated. "You're going to have to hold on to her for a while, Stone, until—"

He slammed his mug down, sloshing hot tea onto his hand. "Wait a minute, Sauvage, we had a deal. You told me this woman would die if I refused this job. You said I was the only one who could get to her in the time frame. You also said you were going to take her off my hands ASAP!"

"I'm sorry. I've had to target all our spare resources elsewhere. You're all I've got out there right now. You can handle one woman, Stone."

Luke swore viciously. "Listen up, Sauvage, I'm not a goddamn babysitter. You're in breach of my contract. I can walk from this—"

"Can you, Stone?" Jacques's voice was cold.

Luke cursed again, dragged his hand over his hair.

"Look, I know what happened to your family in Australia. I know that's why you wanted out. But you're the best in the business and you're all we've got. You can do this."

"Why the hell *should* I?"

"You want to stay on FDS books, don't you?"

Luke was quiet for a moment.

"If you turn her out onto the streets now, the woman dies. It's simple. And it's your call."

Luke closed his eyes. He felt sick to his stomach. This was exactly what he didn't want—sole responsibility for a woman's life. Images of blood seared his brain. He could smell it. He could feel the warm body of his wife in his arms, dying. The blood from the baby. So much blood.

Luke had managed to take care of everyone, except the woman he loved. She'd died pregnant with his child because he'd been too damn busy protecting someone else. His family had been slaughtered because of *him.*

He hadn't wanted to live after that. Almost chose not to. But he hadn't quite found the guts to kill himself.

"Stone?"

Luke inhaled deeply. "Okay," he said coolly, very quietly. "But if I fail, it's on your head." He wasn't taking responsibility on this one. He couldn't. Never again.

"You're still the best at this, Stone," Jacques said, just as quietly. "We both know you are."

"You overestimate me, mate."

"I believe in you. It's why I hired you. It's why I'm asking you to do this now."

Silence.

"And…Stone, try and stay somewhat inside the law, would you? Cooperation with the Canadians is going to be tough enough down the road as it is, especially now that you've engaged the cops."

"I'll do what I can." Luke hit a button and killed the call. He sat back in his chair, eyes closed.

"I'll leave if you want me to."

He jerked to his feet and spun to face Jessica. "Jesus! How long have you been standing there?"

"Long enough to know you want me 'off your hands'…."

He forced air from his lungs with a puff of his cheeks and rubbed his brow hard. "And just where do you think you would you go?"

She shrugged and he noticed suddenly how feminine and vulnerable she looked in his oversized cargo pants, T-shirt and sweater. Her hair was wet and her skin scrubbed to an innocent glow. But it was her eyes and mouth that did him in. There was nothing vulnerable there. They were provocatively sexy as all get-out. He thought about all this woman had endured, what she'd once had in life and what had been taken from her by the Triad. And his heart squeezed sharp and fast. He—if anyone—should understand.

It was a Triad that had taken his wife and child in Australia.

He turned his back on her, stalked into the kitchen and poured a coffee. She accepted it with both hands and a slight bow of the head—a gesture he found both exotic and genuine, endearing.

"You want something to eat?"

She shook her head.

"Okay, then. Lets talk." He pulled out a chair at the dining room table. "Sit."

"I…I don't want to be in your way if—"

He snorted. "If what? Look, I'm sorry you heard that, but understand this: I took the job. And I don't quit something once I sign on."

Only fail. I can still fail.

"Don't worry, I won't fail you, Jess." He had no idea why he said it. But there it was. Some part of him was determined not to let this woman—or himself—down.

"Now sit."

He scooped up the maps and seated himself opposite her.

"I'm going to bring you up to speed. But first priority is for you to tell me how those guys knew you were going to be at that pay phone. Who else knew you were going to call Giles Rehnquist from that booth, at that time?"

Jessica looked into his eyes. "Absolutely no one."

"You must have told some—"

She set her mug down firmly. "I told *no one*."

His brows lowered. "Could someone have overheard? Think. Maybe you—"

"Listen to me, Stone." She couldn't call him Luke, not now, not after what she'd overheard. "Whatever people might say, I am *not* crazy. I'm sick to death of all those knowing, sympathetic glances. I took those photos because I want my life back." Her eyes burned with hot emotion. "And since you're stuck with me now there is one thing you better know about me. Those men may have taken everything they possibly could have from me and they may want to kill me, but I *will not* run from them. I don't run from anything. Ever."

He pursed his lips, nodded slowly, something akin to admiration in his eyes. "Then you're a better person than I, Jessica Chan," he said very quietly.

"What?"

"Nothing. So you believe the only person who knew you were going to be there at that time was Giles?"

"Damn right."

"Why did you call *him?*"

"Because he is—was—a friend, someone I could trust. Giles was the only person who truly believed in what happened to me in Hubei three years ago. He believed the man I call The Chemist exists and is a high-level assassin for a covert faction within the ruling party." She paused, staring at her coffee. "Before my abduction, Giles had been helping me investigate collusion between the Dragon Heads crime syndicate and top officials in the Chinese Communist Party. We had a deal that he could use whatever information I had once I broke the story." She lifted her eyes to his. "Giles knew the players. He understood the government and he knew the workings of the Triad intimately. I needed his advice. *That's* why I called him. He said he'd find a way to help me and he told me to call back in two days, from that same phone at that time. He told me to find an ATM somewhere on the other side of town, withdraw whatever cash I could and use it to find a cheap hotel."

Jessica took a sip of her coffee, welcoming the warmth that diffused through her chest. A distant part of her mind noted that while Luke had made coffee for her, his choice for himself was green tea.

"Is that what you did?"

She nodded. "I found a hotel in Gastown where a single woman renting a room by the night is not unusual. I paid cash upfront and I stayed in that room until it was time to make the call."

"And no one followed you?"

"I don't see how they could have. If they knew I was there they would have come for me earlier, right?"

Luke lowered his brows, studied her. "What about food?"

"I didn't eat."

He nodded slowly, a strange look sifting into his eyes. "You didn't think it strange that Giles made you call back from the exact same phone?"

"I…I guess I did. But I knew he had to have his reasons. He had contacts and I was clean out of options."

"He was CIA, Jess."

She felt her jaw drop. Her whole world tilted and resettled slightly off axis.

"Are you sure?" she asked quietly.

"Dead sure. He wanted a fix on your location while he contacted Langley for direction. He wanted to be sure they could get to you."

She dropped her face into her hands, rubbed her skin. Then looked up. "I…I don't understand."

He opened his mouth to say something, a strange expression in his features. Then he changed his mind, shut his laptop and surged to his feet. "Grab your camera bag, Jess."

"Why?"

"Just do it." He reached for a backpack. "If the conversation you had was exclusively between you and Giles and you're one-hundred percent certain there is no way this information got out from your end, it leaves only one alternative—it got out on Giles's end in Shanghai. And that means we need to move. Fast."

He tossed her a down parka and thick woolen hat then shut his laptop and slid it into his pack along with his satellite phone. He crouched down, unscrewed a bolt under his kitchen table and lifted the top, revealing a large compartment under the surface. He scooped up what looked like different passports and ID's, some license plates, a roll of duct tape, a radio, a scanner, technical field glasses, a knife and rounds of ammunition.

She stared blankly.

"Put the coat on," he barked as he snagged his wallet off the counter.

"Why? Where are we going?"

He took her arm, helping her into the parka. "If Xiang's men were tipped off about the rendezvous at the phone booth, they may also have been tipped off about me. They might know you're here right now, in my house. Until we know what the hell is going on, and how that information got out from Shanghai, we need to go to ground."

"Wait, I don't understand! You're saying *Giles* sold me out?"

"I'm saying there must have been a leak somewhere in the chain—an informant with a direct line to the Triad here in Vancouver."

"But how?"

"I don't know. It's probably what got Giles killed and, until we find that leak, we're sitting ducks, too."

She stood dumbfounded as he grabbed his leather jacket.

"Now, Jess, *move!* They could be here any second."

They shot out the door and fled into the darkness, Luke guiding Jessica over the thick snow that now covered the boardwalk.

Chapter 4

Halyards chinked against frozen masts as they raced down the dock. But just as they reached the stairs that would take them from sea level up to the parking lot, headlights cut round a building, illuminating falling snow. Luke jerked Jessica down into shadow behind a set of pilings.

A black SUV cruised slowly into the parking lot and cut the engine. Luke could hear a second vehicle approaching.

"Quick," he whispered, "back that way."

They ran back along the boardwalk, ducking below a wall just as the beams of a second vehicle swung over their position. They held dead still as the tires of the second vehicle scrunched through snow and came to a stop.

Silence grew deafening as tension pressed down on them and snow began to accumulate on their clothes.

What in hell were they waiting for?

Luke peered cautiously up over the wall, his snow-covered woolen hat providing camouflage. His vehicle was at the far end of the parking lot, behind the two black SUVs. He and Jessica would have to get past them somehow.

The passenger window in the first SUV was suddenly lowered. A match flashed, glowing orange. The scent of cigarette smoke reached him, pungent in the crisp air.

Then the driver's door opened and boots squeaked onto snow. Luke heard snatches of what sounded like Chinese.

"It's a dialect from the south," Jessica whispered against his ear as she tried to peer over the edge and see what he was looking at.

He pushed her back down. "Stay low," he hissed.

He reached into his pack, found his night scopes and trained them on the vehicles. He could make out six Asian men getting out of the cars, all packing serious automatic firepower.

Definitely triad. Somehow they'd gotten an ID on him. This bothered Luke. He rented the boathouse under a false name, paid for everything with credit cards backed by funds from FDS front companies and offshore numbered accounts.

Someone with inside information had to have fingered him directly.

And if the Dragon Heads knew exactly who he was, they had to know he'd taken Jessica and killed two of their men. A contract would be put out on him. Luke knew how these men worked.

Anger welled inside him. This pretty much ended his intellience-gathering gig in this city. Jesus, this was beginning to feel personal.

Jessica edged closer to him, and he could smell his shampoo on her wet hair. "What are they doing?" she whispered.

"Don't know. Stay down," he growled, suddenly—irrationally—angry with *her*.

He watched through his scopes as a third vehicle pulled into the parking lot and drew to a stop alongside the others. Four more men climbed out, assault rifles in hand, black coats fluttering in the cold wind.

Luke felt for his weapon. He had eight rounds in the magazine, one in the firing chamber, spare magazines in his pocket. Still, a 9-mm was no match against the kind of fire-power those guys were packing. His best move was evasion, not engagement.

His muscles burned with tension as he watched the posse cross the parking lot and descend the stairs toward the board-walk. One man remained guard at the base of the stairs and the other nine moved like black ghosts along the snowy boardwalk, making directly for Luke's boathouse.

They would find his house empty within seconds and track their prints through the snow.

"Jess," he whispered urgently. "We need to make a run for it. Now."

She nodded.

He hauled her over the wall and they raced across the parking lot in a crouch, the sound of their footsteps swallowed by snow.

Gunshots suddenly peppered the air.

Luke lunged sideways, forcing Jessica down hard behind his SUV. He dragged her behind the wheel hub, covering her body with his own until he could identify the source of the shots. Another barrage of automatic fire rent the winter air. Luke winced. They were shooting up his place. They had to get out of here.

He reached up, quietly opened the passenger door to his SUV, motioned for her to get in. "The snow cover will shield you once you're in," he whispered.

He crept round to the driver's side, dusted a small hole in the snow that had accumulated on the window, climbed into snow-covered cocoon, and eased the door closed. He watched through the small gap, aggression simmering inside him.

Luke didn't like feeling this way. Taking a job personally was always a bad thing, it threatened the state of numbness he'd perfected over the last four years.

The booze had taken care of the first year after his wife's death.

Then he'd quit drinking, clawing his way back out of moribund self-loathing, and beaten himself back into peak mental and physical shape with such sustained and brutal workouts that sleep had finally returned—the kind of sleep that came without booze. The kind of sleep that didn't allow for thoughts or guilt. Or recurring nightmares.

Maybe in reaching this level of cold command over himself Luke had simply traded one coping mechanism for another, but what the hell—he was doing fine with it. It had saved his life. It had gotten him work with the FDS.

It had gotten him here, to Vancouver.

It had been a way to dull the pain that did not involve the bottom of a whiskey bottle and self-disgust. So why was he *feeling* things now?

He glanced at Jessica. It was her fault. She'd opened some damn Pandora's box inside him.

She was shivering again, her frightened eyes fixed on him. She saw him as her last hope. He clenched his teeth and turned away. But before he could dwell on it, all nine men suddenly swarmed out of his boathouse and raced along the boardwalk toward the parking lot.

He tensed. "What the—"

An explosion *whumped* through air, then another, orange flames bursting out from his boathouse, spreading fast, fueled by some kind of accelerant. It took Luke a nanosecond to process what had just happened. His belongings, his photographs, his yacht, his home—every goddamn thing he owned—had just gone up in a giant ball of fire.

Rage erupted in his belly.

This was more than personal. These men had just declared war on him.

"*Luke!* What's happening?" Jessica leaned over him, trying to see through his peephole. He shoved her away, opening his window wide. "Give me your camera."

"What?"

"Just give it to me!"

He aimed the old Minolta out the window, focused on the fleeing men, clicked, zoomed in closer, clicked again and again, capturing their faces. He switched position and snapped the vehicles, zoomed closer, captured the plates.

He kept clicking as the three SUV's fishtailed wildly out of the snowy parking lot and sped away. Fire alarms began to clang as flames crackled and popped. Another gut-hollowing *whoosh* sent shock waves through the air as the diesel fuel containers of his boat caught fire and blew.

Sirens began to scream. People raced out of the other boathouses, black silhouettes against white snow and hot raw flames, some diving into the frigid water to escape the blaze.

Staff and guests flocked from the nearby Granville Island Hotel. More alarms sounded as the fire spread quickly to the adjacent art school and another row of boats. More yachts exploded in balls of fire. Bedlam engulfed the island as Luke silently handed Jessica her camera and started the engine.

"Are you strapped in?" His voice was tight.

She fumbled with the buckle and once he saw she was secure, he flipped on the windshield wipers and hit the gas. He swerved out of the parking lot, racing away from the scene as an army of fire engines, ambulances and police vehicles converged on the pandemonium behind them.

Luke slowed his vehicle as they approached the bridge on-ramp. Snow was turning to slush and it would be light in a few hours. They needed to get out of the city before that happened.

"What now?" she asked in a thin voice.

He inhaled deeply, wishing he'd never met her. "Now," he said flatly, "we really are in the same boat, Jess."

"Where are we going?" He could hear despair in her voice and guilt stirred in him.

"Someplace out of the city," he said. "Somewhere I can hand you over to the CIA before—" he cut it. Fell silent.

"Before I do any more damage. That's what you were going to say, wasn't it?"

"The damage is done, Jess. There's no going back. Now we deal with the road ahead. Together." *Unfortunately.*

And he was going to make sure he got it over with as quickly as possible, he thought as he cranked up the heater to warm her.

"I'm sorry," she said.

His eyes cut sharply to hers and he saw the telltale glisten of tears. He looked away quickly. He really needed to get away from her soon. Before he let her down. Before he let himself down.

"Dry your hair," he said curtly in an effort to distract her. "Turn up the fan on your side."

He pulled off the road about twenty minutes later, just before they hit the notorious Sea to Sky Highway, and changed the license plates.

Jessica studied Luke's profile as he fiddled with the car radio. The meteorologist was warning of three back-to-back storm fronts, the first of which would hit within the hour. It was almost seven in the morning, yet the sky was still an ominous black. Already a mounting wind was buffeting their vehicle as they negotiated the twisting road that hugged cliffs above a sheer drop to the ocean.

Luke hadn't said a word since they'd hit this dangerous stretch of road, but Jessica could sense the anger rolling off him in waves. She felt absolutely terrible that he'd lost his house. She was especially torn by the destruction of those haunting black-and-white images that had graced his walls.

"Luke, I really am sorry for the loss of your home," she said, unable to stop herself.

His hands tightened on the wheel. "Don't be," he said. "Not your fault."

"It is my fault. If it wasn't for me, Stephanie and Giles would be alive, you'd still have your—"

"You're thinking like a victim, Jess." His voice was clipped. "You did nothing to deserve this."

"Well, neither did you. So I *am* sorry."

A muscle began to pulse at his jawline. "Quit apologizing. I told you, it's my job."

"It was also your *home,* Luke."

His eyes cut to hers. "Forget about it, okay? It was just stuff. You don't get to put down roots in my business. You don't get attached to *stuff.*" He blew out a breath. "Look, Jess, it was a mistake to accumulate what I had. Mistakes happen when you get complacent. This was simply a wake-up call. That's all."

Jessica had a sense Luke was anything but complacent. And something about his home told her he did care about what was in it. She trusted her instincts. They'd given her many a scoop in the past.

"How long had you been living there, Luke?" she asked quietly.

"Long enough."

"So why did you come to Vancouver?"

He remained silent.

She shifted in her seat to face him. "Look, if you just spit it out and tell me who I'm dealing with here, then I'll leave you alone, okay?"

Again, his silence was almost threatening.

"If you were in my shoes, Luke, you'd ask. You'd need to know."

"Fair enough," he said, glancing at her. "The FDS sent me here to establish a small satellite office for gathering Pacific Rim intelligence, specifically on Asian criminal networks that collude with terrorists."

"I thought you said your company was a private military company."

"It is. PMCs are moving increasingly into the intelligence field. Clients demand this service."

"Why Vancouver?"

"That should be obvious—it's a major port city on the Pacific Rim with a significant Asian population and it's an easy entry point to the United States."

"You're gathering this intelligence yourself?"

"My job is—*was*," he corrected, "to get a handle on the key players behind the local tongs and triads and to determine what sort of new businesses they're moving into. Traditionally it's been heroin, gambling, extortion, black-market weapons, human trafficking and business and banking fraud. However, the syndicates are moving into increasingly sophisticated cor-porate espionage and, along with military hardware components, they're now trafficking in biological and chemical components. I was supposed to assess which groups have the potential to become real political problems."

"Are the Dragon Heads part of this?"

"The Dragon Heads Triad is at the top of my list. They're one of the primary reasons I'm here. They've been aggressively acquiring territory around the world by usurping long-established gangs and networks. They infiltrate the rival tong or triad, then assassinate the leaders and govern by a code of terror. Anyone who steps out of line is killed as a warning."

"You say this *was* your job?"

He snorted. "I suspect I'm going to have trouble fulfilling those functions now that I'm on the Dragon Heads hit list."

Jessica's stomach twisted. This just kept getting worse. "What makes you a specialist in this area, Luke?"

"Let's just say I've had some…personal experience with triads."

She thought about the scars on his back. "Is that why they sent you to pick me up?"

"No, Jess. I was the only mutt available. I just happen to also have significant close-protection experience."

"Luke?"

He glanced at her again. "What?"

"I heard you say on the phone that you'd refused to do bodyguard gigs for this company of yours."

"Yes."

"Did…something happen on a job? Back in Australia?"

His energy shifted perceptibly. "Does this kind of interrogation come naturally from being an investigative journalist, Jessica, or were you just born nosy?"

She smiled in spite of herself. "I get the message. You don't want to talk about yourself."

"Right."

She leaned back into her seat and closed her eyes, fatigue starting to consume her again as the adrenaline wore off. "But I will tell you one thing about me, Luke Stone," she said softly through closed eyes. "In the end I always get the information I want."

Luke felt a smile tug at his lips. She'd just issued him a challenge, almost playful in spite of the situation. It awakened something in him. Something that felt very, very foreign.

"That dogged curiosity is exactly what got you in trouble in the first place, Jessica Chan," he said. "A lesser person would have given up after what you'd been through."

Like he had.

She opened one eye. "Was that a compliment, Stone?"

"Just a statement of fact, Jess."

"You do realize you've been calling me 'Jess' from the moment I met you? Is that an Australian thing or were you just born irreverent?"

He chuckled softly, caught off guard. He liked this woman. She had a way of opening him up. But that was exactly the *problem* with her. It made her dangerous to him, because Luke didn't want to go back to being the man he once was. He didn't want to open himself to emotion.

She closed her eyes again. "Your laugh almost makes you sound friendly," she murmured.

"Me?"

"Comes as a shock, does it, Stone?"

It did, actually. He didn't think of himself that way—as nice. Mostly he tried to avoid people. A bluntness bordering on rude usually did the job. His aggressive physical appearance took care of the rest.

He stole a quick look at her.

She'd fallen asleep, lashes dark on pale cheeks, her exhalations soft. An odd feeling quirked through his chest as he looked at her.

Luke returned his focus to the road. The wind was increasing, small flakes of snow were once again hitting the windshield as they drove into the brunt of the new storm.

But while the weather was foul outside, listening to her sleeping next to him felt warm, intimate, and Luke couldn't help thinking about what she'd just said.

Friendly? *Him?*

He felt his lips twitching into a smile. The idea was amusing, strange, like the taste of something new.

Didn't taste too hellish, either.

As they neared Furry Creek, driving snow was settling alarmingly fast on the road. A sedan in front of them skidded sideways, slumping nose first into a ditch at the base of a rock face held back with wire, red taillights upended. Luke glanced at Jessica. She was still fast asleep.

He looked up into the rearview mirror. A vehicle behind him was stopping to aid the driver. Luke kept driving. It was safer to avoid stopping. Stopping might mean engaging police.

But less than one minute later, he saw it was futile. Up ahead lay a police roadblock, luminous pink flares lining the road where Mounties in reflective gear waved certain vehicles off the road with flashlights.

He cursed, wondering what they were looking for. They shouldn't have an ID on him personally, and he'd changed plates. The RCMP out here also would not likely know about Jessica's link to the murder of Stephanie Ward—that was Vancouver P.D. jurisdiction.

As they hit a bump, Jessica woke, rubbed her face, then sat bolt upright. "A roadblock? They're looking for us. Turn around, Luke."

"We can't. Not without being obvious." His brain ticked over fast as they approached. "Jess," he said urgently. "You never told me how the Triad knew you had taken those photos in the first place."

"I don't *know!* I told only the RCMP. That very same night, my apartment was ransacked." She ran a hand through her hair, then looked at him. "Luke, they must have had an informant in the police."

He had to think fast. "Don't say anything," he said, eyes fixed on the roadblock ahead. "Pretend you're still asleep, put that hat on, turn your face away." Luke slowed the vehicle as he lowered the window. A gust of flakes swirled into the warm interior.

A cop walked over, bent down, a layer of snow thick on the peak of his hat. "Good morning, sir," he said as he directed his flashlight at Luke, then panned over to Jessica.

Chapter 5

"Is there a problem, Officer?" Luke asked.

"We're doing a vehicle check, sir, not permitting anyone through without proper snow tires and chains. There's heavy weather ahead. Road north of Pemberton is closed due to an avalanche and we're expecting worse over the next seventy-two hours."

"We're equipped."

"Where are you headed, sir?"

Luke frowned inwardly. This wasn't standard. "Only as far as Squamish," he lied.

"Can I see your license, please?"

Luke offered one with an alias. The officer went back to his vehicle to check it.

Luke sat calmly. The false ID would hold, but he didn't like the fact it was being checked at all. The cop returned, did a walk around the vehicle, noting tires.

"You carrying chains, sir?"

"Yes, like I said, we're equipped."

The cop handed the license back. "There's no guarantee the road will stay open north of Squamish if the weather worsens."

"As I said, officer, we're not going that far."

The cop nodded. "Have a good day, then, sir." He stepped back and waved another car over behind them.

Luke edged his vehicle forward, tires slipping slightly.

"Thank God," Jessica whispered as she sat up. "I thought they were hunting for us."

"They are. They just haven't connected the dots yet."

Moisture filled her eyes and she looked away quickly. Luke's heart punched. He placed his hand on her knee. "It's okay, Jess. We'll get you through this."

He had no business making promises he might not be able to keep. But he'd be damned if he wasn't going to try and make her feel better.

"Thank you," she whispered, barely audibly, covering his hand lightly with hers. Electricity sparked through Luke's arm at the contact. Shocked, he withdrew his hand instantly. His tires were slipping, he needed both hands on the wheel, full attention on the road ahead.

Dawn arrived in pale monochromatic grays, a diaphanous curtain of snowflakes separating from the dark underbellies of clouds that socked low over the mountains. All around them granite cliffs were fringed with ridges of conifers that speared aggressively into the sky.

Luke pulled off the highway and turned into the village of Squamish. "Breakfast?" he asked.

She blew out a lungful of air and smiled shakily. "You have absolutely no idea how good that sounds right now."

He'd made her happy and the simple satisfaction that gave him was startling. It had been an awfully long time since he'd felt a need to make someone else happy. "I'm afraid it has to be the drive-through."

"What? They have green tea?" she said with feigned surprise.

He shot her a mock scowl. "You're perceptive for someone terrified out of her wits."

"Hard not to notice a guy like you drinking tea, Luke. Is it necessity or vanity?"

"Meaning?"

"Meaning, do you need to stay in peak health for your job or do you just like a honed body?"

He forced a laugh and left it at that. But she'd hit a sore point and he suspected Jessica knew it. Because for Luke, having an iron-willed control over both mind and body was a matter of pure survival, in more ways than one.

After hitting a fast-food restaurant, they ate in the parking lot, listening to highway updates on the radio, running the engine to keep warm. According to the radio, the road north was a complete mess, cars going off all over the place. Anyone without proper snow tires and chains was being turned around at Alice Lake.

"That's the logical turnaround point," said Luke, nodding toward the radio as he chewed. "Those cops back at Furry Creek were looking for something else. Probably the Granville Island Bombers."

Jessica blew steam from her hot coffee, cradling her cup in both hands. "But you don't think they've connected the Gastown shootings to the Granville Island fire—and us?"

"Not yet," he said reaching for his tea. "That Mountie got a damn good look of our faces. If he'd been acting off any kind of physical description, we wouldn't be sitting here right now. They likely have descriptions of the cars and plates seen fleeing the fire scene and he was probably watching for a vehicle like mine, but the plate didn't match. Good thing we changed ours."

Jessica studied his unyielding profile as he sipped his tea. Nothing fazed this guy and his rock-solid confidence relaxed her a little.

"But wouldn't they still be looking for you specifically?" she asked. "I mean, it was your place that went up in flames."

He shook his head. "I used covers, aliases, offshore accounts for rental payments and purchases, that sort of thing. It'll take forensic investigators forever to sift through the carnage and determine I wasn't even in the boathouse when it went up in flames. It'll take them even longer to match the occupant to me. If they ever do."

She stared at him. "You weren't kidding about not putting down roots, were you?"

"The more attached you are, the more you stand to lose," he said. "And having something to lose opens you to manipulation. You give your enemy an edge."

"Must play havoc with relationships."

He slid his eyes over and met hers. "That the journalist at work again?"

She shrugged. "Just me being curious."

He studied her for a beat. "I don't do relationships. So it's not a problem." He swigged back the rest of his tea and crunched the cup in his hand. "I need to check in with the FDS. Wait here."

He got out, dumped the fast-food bag in the garbage and strode across the parking lot while speaking on his satellite phone. He clearly didn't want her to hear.

Jessica watched him through blowing snow, flakes settling on the ruff of his jacket and on his hair. He looked rugged, distant. Cool. Like his photographs. He reminded her of something off the cover of National Geographic—one of those untouchable men who were as wild and craggy as the mountains they climbed. Dangerous if you misstepped, but solid and life-supporting in other ways.

Jessica liked to think she was an astute judge of character, but she couldn't quite pin this guy down. And then there was the fact she'd trusted Giles implicitly. Not in her wildest dreams would she have suspected he was CIA, perhaps even using the information she was digging up on government collusion for his own covert purposes. It could even have been her association with Giles that led the Chinese to think she was a spy. Giles could have been the reason she was abducted, her life destroyed. She felt ill at the thought.

Had she the missed warning signs back then? Was she missing them now?

Was she so desperate to lean on Luke Stone because she was so damned lonely and frightened?

Truth was, she didn't really have a choice.

Luke Stone was all she had.

Luke paced the length of a snowbank as he briefed Jacques on the firebombing. "My personal details were leaked to the Triad," he said. "How in hell did that happen?"

"No one apart from us and a very narrow CIA circle knows you're on this job, Stone. You must have been tailed."

"Not a chance. Someone gave out my information. They came directly for me."

"We'll look into it."

"Tell me—how did Giles Rehnquist die?"

"He was assassinated, gang style."

"Triad?"

"It looks that way."

"And he was killed right after he got a call from Jessica Chan?"

"Right after he informed his CIA handler that Jessica Chan had seen and photographed Xiang-Li and the man she calls The Chemist."

"So there *is* a leak."

"There appears to have been some breach in CIA security from the Shanghai end, and that's why Weston contracted us to bring Chan in. He wants to appear objective while he deals with the breach. He's also closed the circle on this. Your personal details should be secure."

"Well, they're not. Let me get this straight. Rehnquist calls his handler to tell him Jessica Chan has just photographed Xiang-Li and The Chemist in Vancouver. But up until now the U.S. diplomatic position has been that The Chemist doesn't even exit. Why does the CIA suddenly want her testimony against him now?"

"I'm not privy to that, Stone. Our contract is simply to bring her in."

"I don't like it. Too many loose ends. The Dragon Heads moved on Jessica *before* she even called Rehnquist in Shanghai. They went for her right after she approached the RCMP. Somehow the information about her photos went straight from the RCMP to the Dragon Heads. And then when she contacted Rehnquist for help, he was assassinated? Something's off here, Sauvage. The leak is not just on the Shanghai end."

"We're looking into it, Stone. You just look after your principal. We've arranged for a CIA pickup at the airfield in Pemberton, about 60 miles north of your current location, weather permitting. Forecast says we should have a break between the two fronts. You need to get her to the drop point by 9:00 a.m. tomorrow morning. If anything changes, I'll let you know ASAP."

"Right." Luke started pacing again, snow gusting at him as the storm closed in.

"And Stone, tell me where you will be staying tonight as soon as you know."

The phone went dead.

Luke cursed and kicked at the snowbank, pissed off for more reasons than one. He was steamed at Jacques for landing him with this job in the first place, mad at himself for the way he was reacting to it and annoyed with Jessica for…just being gorgeous and smart. And brave.

And so damn likeable.

He got back into the car with a stubborn set to his jaw and flint in his eyes. "Right," he said curtly. "I've updated Jacques— told him we're going to drive as far north in this weather as we can. Meantime the CIA is arranging a chopper to pick you up at the Pemberton airfield tomorrow. We just need to hole up for the night, then we rendezvous with them in the morning and I hand you over." He started the ignition, and shifted the car into gear.

Panic whipped through Jessica.

"What will *you* do once you've handed me over?"

He shrugged. "Get out of the country for a while. Take another offshore contract." He turned onto the highway and they drove in uncomfortable silence, deeper into the storm and higher into the ragged mountain range.

Langley. CIA headquarters

CIA director Blake Weston hung up the phone and pinched the bridge of his nose, relieved to learn FDS still had Jessica Chan. By tomorrow night he could conceivably have her in Washington D.C., her photographs developed and CIA labs running biometrics technology against databases. Then he could arrange for her to disappear in an agency protection program. At least, that was how he wanted his intentions to appear.

But Blake had other plans for the woman. It would be best if she were eliminated before she entered the United States.

He stood up, opened his bottle of antacids and tipped several into his palm.

Jessica Chan's photographs could launch a Sino-American cold war and change the face of global politics for the foreseeable future.

No one wanted trouble with China on their hands. Especially not him.

Those photographs had to be destroyed along with her.

Her bodyguard would need to be eliminated, as well. It was unfortunate they didn't die in the boathouse bombing like they were supposed to.

Blake swallowed his pills, then flipped open his cell phone.

There was no traffic on the road now, just pristine snowy wilderness forcing them to drive slower and slower.

Luke hadn't spoken a word for close to twenty minutes when he finally said, "I want you tell me about your abduction."

Jessica was surprised. "Why? You saw my dossier. It's all in there."

He shook his head. "I'm missing something. Things are not adding up. I need to hear it from you."

She exhaled heavily, turned to look out the window at the

white forest blurred by driving snow. China suddenly felt so very remote and she preferred to keep it that way.

"You said you were investigating the possibility the Dragon Heads are being controlled by a hard-line covert arm of the ruling Chinese Communist Party."

"They are," she muttered.

"You ever find proof?"

She sighed. "You know I didn't."

"And Giles Rehnquist knew what you were doing? He supported you? He believed in this collusion?"

"Yes. He was the one who gave me the tip that led to my kidnapping. He told me he'd heard a top government official was meeting a top Dragon Heads member at a restaurant in Shanghai's business district." She sighed. "I guess knowing he was CIA puts a whole new spin on it now."

"Tell me about the actual abduction. What happened?"

She moistened her mouth. "I went to the business district, hoping to catch sight of the meet—"

"You didn't think it odd that these men would meet in the open?"

"Not really. The government has long turned a blind eye to the triad culture and there is often communication between triad business leaders and officials. It was more a matter of *who* was meeting who that day. I was trying to build a file, find proof that there was actually a coordinated and concerted effort to push a covert and hard-line Chinese Communist Party agenda around the world, using the Dragon Heads network. I wanted to show they were becoming aggressively organized."

"And that's when you were snatched?"

"A car pulled up alongside me on the sidewalk. I had a sack thrust over my head and was bundled into the vehicle."

"No witnesses?"

She shook her head. "There never are in China. People are terrified of coming forward."

"And they took you to the interior?"

"I was drugged. I woke up in an old warehouse in Hubei

province," she said tonelessly. "I was held there for about two weeks, strapped into some kind of metal chair, rigged up to monitoring equipment. They accused me of being a spy for the United States and injected me with what they said was truth serum. They wanted information, contacts, the names of other agents working in China. They subjected me to physical torture. Denied me water. I got dehydrated, delirious, began hallucinating really badly." She paused, the horror slowly starting to unfurl inside her again no matter how calmly she tried to recite her story. "I…I had to fight just to keep conscious. They brought in a translator who interrogated me in English while they correspondingly ramped up the drug dose, and my hallucinations got worse. I gathered they were collecting data on the performance of the serum, in addition to trying to get information out of me. I pretended I could speak barely any Chinese at all, that I was totally out of it."

"It was probably Giles Rehnquist they were really after," he said. "They may have received a tip that there was a spy at a Shanghai news agency and assumed it was you since you were investigating them."

Jessica looked away. She hated to think that all this time Giles could have stood up for her. The CIA had known all along that what she'd endured was real, yet they'd left her—an innocent—to blow in the wind rather than expose their Chinese operations.

"And it was the man you call The Chemist who administered these hallucinogens?"

She nodded, her mouth dry. "Yes. At the instruction of Dragon Heads boss, Xiang-Li, and a man named Zhenzong Shi, who works for China's Ministry of State Security. He was also there."

Luke's brow furrowed. "You remember this clearly."

Frustration swelled in her. "Yes, dammit, Luke. I *remember!* You sound just like the rest of them!"

"Easy, Jess. Tell me about The Chemist."

She scrubbed her hands over her face. "From what I could piece together, he heads up the manufacture of chemical and biological agents at a government-sponsored lab in Hubei. His chemical compounds have been tested in mass killings of innocent Chinese nationals. It was his nerve gas that killed 75 workers who rioted at a toy factory in the Yangtze Delta."

"How do you know this?"

"I heard them talk about it while they were holding me."

"The Chinese have categorically denied that incident."

"Of course they deny it!" she said through gritted teeth. "Just as they flatly denied what I had endured in that warehouse. Beijing made an official statement saying that The Chemist was a fabrication of my crazy hallucinations."

"But they do admit you were kidnapped, and drugged."

"Well, they couldn't exactly deny *that,* could they? They just claimed it was criminals who abducted and drugged me. They said they had no knowledge of why and that the police had done everything in their power to apprehend them, that all leads just happened to have run dry."

Emotion welled from deep inside Jessica. She opened his glove compartment and rummaged around in it furiously. "Don't you have any tissues in here?" she snapped.

He calmly handed her a clean cotton handkerchief. Jessica took it, hesitated, then blew her nose. "I'm sorry," she said, stiffly. "I don't like talking about it."

He placed his hand on her knee. "I know."

Luke drove in silence, clearly not wanting to push her anymore, which more than anything touched Jessica. She blew her nose again and took a deep breath, determined to follow this through. "The Beijing government said Xiang-Li and their ministry official, Zhenzong Shi, did not know each other—they presented photographic 'proof' from surveillance cameras that Xiang-Li was at a casino in Macau, and Zhenzong Shi in Taiwan, at the time of my abduction."

"They faked the photos."

She laughed bitterly. "Of course they faked them. But who was going to believe me? I was a psychological mess. In the end, Beijing said my abduction was in no way political, and that it was impossible to believe anything I said because of my mental state. Embassy officials, worried about preserving sensitive trade talks, nodded at each other politely and that was that." She glared at him, her pulse thudding at the memories.

The SUV suddenly skidded sideways as Luke rounded a curve. He gripped the wheel, steering carefully into the skid, slowing the vehicle as he edged it back onto the road. Jessica watched his hands on the wheel, noticing them properly for the first time. Rugged and beautiful hands. Tanned. Strong.

"And what convinces you The Chemist is an assassin?" he said, as if the near-accident had never happened.

"I heard them talking. Like I said, they didn't know I was fluent in several Chinese dialects and they thought I was unconscious at that point. Besides, they were going to kill me anyway when they finally realized I wasn't a spy. They became less guarded in what they were saying."

"How did you escape, Jess?"

"I feigned unconsciousness and while they argued in the next room about how to dispose of me that night, I crawled out of a warehouse window." She took a deep breath. "I lay delirious in rice paddies for two days, until some farmers helped me onto a produce truck that took me back to Shanghai where I collapsed in front of the British Embassy." Jessica shuddered involuntarily as the media images flooded back to haunt her—pictures of her curled-up body in the street, needle marks covering her limbs, hair so matted it had to be cut off. "How I was found is pretty well documented in media archives," she said. "The embassy took up my cause, as did the BBC and various journalist associations who had spearheaded the search for me. But with no actual proof, things just fizzled out. And at that point I was too much of a psychological mess to actually help my own cause."

"Plus trade and military talks with China were extremely sensitive at that juncture," said Luke. "It was easier to sweep you under the carpet and avoid political ramifications."

She nodded, going ice-cold again at the thought of the hospitals and years of psychiatric treatment she'd endured after that. "That was really just the *beginning* of my nightmare," she said very quietly. "It's why I came to Vancouver. To start over. If I can break this story, Luke, if I can finally prove what happened in Hubei and implicate Beijing in the cover-up, I'll be able to buy back everything I lost. I will regain my credibility. My pride. Maybe even my job."

He shot her a long, hard, soul-searching look. "Jess, you *do* know the CIA is going to take that film from you."

Her stomach tightened. "That doesn't mean I can't use the images. They're mine. Once the CIA has identified the men, the photos will be in the public domain, anyway."

Luke swallowed, avoiding her eyes. "Not necessarily, Jess. These things—"

"Have a way of being swept under diplomatic carpets," she said bitterly. "Is that what you're telling me?"

"Jess, you know how it works. This is big. They've arranged to get you into a witness protection program—"

She leaned forward, suddenly very angry. "Yeah, Luke. I know how it works! You deliver me like an executioner. Except this time I lose *everything*, including my identity." She slumped back into the seat. She hadn't wanted to admit it to herself, but there was never going to be a story.

She was never going to get her job or her life back.

Not if she went into witness protection.

He pulled off the road suddenly, sliding to a soft halt in a thick drift. "I need to put the chains on," he said. "Want to help?"

Luke showed Jessica how to lay the chains out on the snow and wrap them over the wheels. Fingers cold, she worked in silence alongside him, comforted by the occasional touch of his body against hers as the falling snow wrapped them in a private world. Jessica stole a glance at him, snowflakes settling on his hair, his eyes haunting gray in this light, his features even more rugged. She suspected he'd gotten her out of the car to help her shift mental gear. Once again she was struck by the gentleness in this rough-looking man.

But when he glanced up at her from where he was crouched at the rear wheel, his features remained cool and uncompromising.

"You know what puzzles me?" he said. "You shouldn't be alive."

"I beg your pardon?"

He stood up, dusting snow from his pants. "If your abduction was a Dragon Heads operation—"

"It was."

"Well, then, Dragon Heads codes dictate they should have hunted you down and eliminated you, even in the U.K. They could easily have gotten to you in the hospital."

"Wow, I love the way you put that."

His eyes narrowed onto her. "Why didn't they?"

Jessica shrugged. "I don't know. Maybe they figured no one would ever take me seriously anyway. Maybe coming after me at that point would only have validated my claims."

"I don't buy it."

"Does this mean you don't believe me?"

"Nope," he said opening her door. "It just means things still aren't adding up, that's all."

He placed his hand at the small of her back, guiding her into the car, the compassion in his touch once again at odds with the hard tone in his voice and eyes.

He got in and started the ignition. "My other question is, why are a Chinese government assassin and a triad kingpin in North America now?" He edged the car forward before getting back out and securing the clips on the chains.

He climbed back into the SUV, shut his door. "Whatever they're doing here, they need to keep it secret and that's why they want you dead," he shifted the car into gear, edging carefully back onto the slick highway.

"You sure know how to make a girl feel secure, you know that, Stone?"

The chains rattled and clunked, forcing them to drive at a

snail's pace. He slid his eyes over to her and she saw a slight twinkle in his eyes. "Let's hope we're still moving faster than they are, huh? Nothing like a slow-speed chase to ratchet the tension a little."

Laughter burst spontaneously from her, instantly relieving some of her anxiety.

"Looks good on you," he said as she wiped unexpected tears of mirth from her eyes.

She stilled, hand in midair. "What does?"

"Laughing."

"Yeah?"

"Yeah."

"Maybe you should try it yourself, Stone."

"I'm a little rusty."

"No, really?" she said with a teasing smile. "I'd never have noticed."

Luke felt himself smile. Suddenly, he wanted nothing more than to see her break her big story. And he wanted to help her get it. But that was not his mission.

His mission was pretty much to ensure she never did.

Chapter 6

They were nearing the small ski town of Whistler. In less than an hour they'd be in Pemberton. Their end point.

Jessica saw the road signs and tensed visibly. Luke felt bad for her but said nothing. He needed to mentally prepare to hand her over.

"Will the FDS try to find out why The Chemist and Xiang-Li are in North America?" she asked, her voice somehow smaller.

"That's not our mission, Jess."

She turned to him. "So once you hand me over, your job is done. Just like that. Never look back."

"That's pretty much how it goes."

"If they put me in a CIA protection program it means I'll disappear as Jessica Chan, you do know that? I'll be forced to give up everything that defines me. I'll never get to break my story."

"It'll keep you alive."

"It means I'll never see my mother again."

Luke tightened his grip on the wheel, concentrating on the road. And on avoiding her eyes.

He desperately wanted to say something, anything to make her believe it wasn't so. He knew from Jessica's file that her mother lived near London. There was nothing in the dossier about a father, though. He wanted to ask her about that, but he maintained his silence. His distance. He'd gotten much too close for comfort already.

"You don't care too much about anything, do you?" she snapped suddenly.

His eyes whipped to hers, something hotly volatile sparking inside him. He gripped the wheel tighter. "No, Jess. I don't."

Her mouth flattened. "I don't want to go into witness protection."

He said nothing.

"I don't want to live like that."

Anger, refusal to feel, churned violently against the empathy mounting in Luke. "What the hell do you want, then?" he said through clenched teeth.

"I…I…don't know." He heard the wobble in her voice, then her deep, steadying breath.

"I…want to *crush* them."

His eyes whipped to hers. "You *what?*"

"The Chemist, the Dragon Heads, the covert arm of the Chinese Communist Party—I want to take them all down. I want whatever is going on exposed, splashed all over the bloody world media, slammed into the public eye. I want it over. If they're behind bars, if the Chinese government is exposed, if foreign governments and the United Nations get onto this, then I can be *me*—Jessica Chan." She gritted her teeth. "I don't want to run. I don't want to hide. I am not a quitter."

Inexplicable guilt crashed through Luke.

This woman put him to shame. It made the independence, the isolation he treasured and fought so hard to maintain seem suddenly so trite, selfish. Cold.

Weak, even.

He'd rebuilt his life by running. From himself. From emotion. While she'd been trying to rebuild hers by hitting back. Facing it all.

He shook his head. Jessica Chan was something else. Her exotic eyes. Her raw energy. Her courage in the face of fear. It was flat-out sexy. It turned him on in spite of himself. A warm energy rode up from somewhere deep inside him, fueling a drive to tap into her fire, into life. To help her.

She was beginning to make him feel that handing her over would be…defeat.

Suddenly Luke saw the future forking in front of him, and he was being forced to pick a road. The heart of a renegade began to beat softly within him, growing louder, harder with each second. What did he have to lose, anyway?

His life's possessions had gone up in flames. And he'd lost what really mattered a long time ago.

He swerved off the road suddenly, taking the turnoff into Whistler.

"Where are you going?"

"We'll get your film developed here," he said quietly. "I'll send copies to Jacques. Maybe his team can ID The Chemist."

Dumbfounded, she stared at him. "I…thought that wasn't your mission."

Grimly, he glanced her way. "What the CIA doesn't know won't hurt us."

Jacques wasn't going to like this one bit, thought Luke as he drove to the secluded upper village area at the base of Blackcomb Mountain. But his rash decision made him feel somehow alive. Engaged. Even though he knew that investing himself in this woman's fight couldn't be anything but lose-lose in the end, he wasn't able to stop himself. Something about Jessica Chan had irrevocably touched him.

"I've used this camera store before, for my backcountry trips," he said as he parked up against a massive snowbank. "My appearance here won't throw up any red flags."

Jessica rolled her film on, opened her Minolta and popped the spool out. "This is the only proof I have left," she said as she handed it to him. Luke noticed her hands trembled.

He looked up into her eyes. "You're nervous?"

"I…I just have this irrational fear that…maybe the photos won't come out, that maybe there's nothing on there."

A cool whisper of doubt threaded through Luke. "But the other ones came out fine, right?" He'd never seen them. No one had. They had only her word.

"Yes."

And then they disappeared.

He leaned forward. "Jess, you *did* see those guys in Chinatown, didn't you?"

She looked pale as a ghost suddenly. "Of course I saw them. It's just…"

"That you're afraid you might be hallucinating again?"

She looked away. "I'm always afraid, Luke."

He cupped the side of her face and turned her back to meet his eyes. "Don't be."

She swallowed. "I was diagnosed as paranoid schizophrenic. People like that lose touch with reality."

"It was pharmacologically induced, Jess. You're in control now, remember that."

"Doctors said severe stress could induce a relapse."

Luke frowned inwardly. Could it actually be possible she'd fabricated the entire thing? He hated himself for even entertaining the idea but he *had* read her dossier. She'd endured a severe hallucinatory period for well over a year, with several relapses the following year. Perhaps she'd had another relapse.

He forced a smile, held up the canister. "It'll *all* be in here. Have faith."

"I *don't* have faith, Luke. That's why I started taking photographs in the first place—just to prove my memories of each day were real."

He nodded slowly. "I know." She needed this proof. Badly.

Not just to nail the Dragon Heads. She needed it for her own
sanity. She also needed some decent food and sleep. "Wait
here, I'll be right back."

"I'm coming with you," she said, opening her door

"Jess, no. They have security cameras in there."

"I'll wait outside the shop, then. I'm not sitting here doing
nothing. I just *can't*. There are tons of tourists out there, no one
is going to notice me among them."

"Jessica, please. I don't want those camera guys associat-
ing your face in any way with this film."

Her mouth tightened.

He touched her face again and smiled. "It'll be okay, I
promise." And he hated himself for making yet another promise
he wasn't sure he could keep.

Luke pushed open the store door, the tinkle of a bell an-
nouncing his entrance as the scent of darkroom chemicals and
computers combined with heat assailed him. He handed the
technician the roll of film, asked for a rush job—develop and
scan to digital.

The tech told him it was no problem and he said he'd wait.

But as Luke watched the technician an unexpected tension
began to mount in him and he realized he was consciously
willing her images to be there—not for the mission, not for the
CIA, nor the FDS, but for Jessica.

He didn't want this one little thing to break her, because he
knew it could. Her camera had been her therapy. He'd read that
in her dossier. Her photographs had rebuilt her confidence in
her own memories, and he'd hate to see that utterly destroyed
now by a roll of film that had nothing on it apart from the photos
he'd shot at the firebombing scene.

Alarmed, Luke realized his urge to protect Jessica had
deepened to a point well beyond his mission.

The job he hadn't wanted was becoming one he was going
to have trouble letting go.

* * *

Jessica watched skiers and snowboarders clunk past the car, cumbersome boots giving them an awkward alien gait, their pink-cheeked exhilaration tangible.

A couple of skiers about her own age laughed as they passed her window and Jessica's chest suddenly felt indescribably hollow.

The entire village had the ambience of a festive holiday season and it reminded her it was almost the Chinese new year. That made her think of her mother. Her sense of isolation deepened.

Farther afield, people wrapped in jackets and scarves sat under propane heaters on café patios nursing coffees and aperitifs. In front of the patio a ski patroller's border collie chased snowballs that kids threw for him. One *whooshed* out of left field and *thunked* the patroller in the head. The kids squealed and the dog yipped like crazy searching for the vanished snowball at his feet. Jessica smiled in spite of herself.

Must be nice to actually have a life, she thought. And a dog. It seemed such a normal thing. She wished she could be normal.

Who was she kidding? Her life hadn't been normal from the moment that hood had been thrust over her head.

Bitterness filled Jessica. And she was so tired of feeling bitter. It was a destructive emotion. She wanted something different. She wanted what those people out there in the village had. And that film Luke was developing in the store was her very last shot to get it.

He was taking forever. What if there were no images?

What if they screwed up the developing process, destroyed the film and no one believed her? Desperation flushed through her. Damn, she wanted to barge in there and develop the film herself. Just to make sure. She tried to calm herself, but she couldn't take the waiting anymore.

She pulled the wool hat low over her head, left the car and trudged through the snow toward the store. Bells chinked as she shoved open the door.

Luke whirled round, his hand going for the gun holstered at his back. He saw it was her and froze, eyes lancing into her like cold metal razors. The warning in them stopped Jessica dead in her tracks.

Fear trickled down through her impatience.

She swallowed, backing slowly toward the door, a vague anger beginning to simmer under the fear. Yet she exited obediently and waited outside.

Luke took the CD from the technician, paid in cash, thanked the man and watched over the counter to ensure the digital files were properly deleted from the system as he'd requested.

Then he spun round, pushed through the door and stalked straight past Jessica. She had to run to keep up.

"Luke!"

He got back into the car, slammed the door. She climbed in after him, slammed her own door. His eyes bored into hers. "Do that one more time—disobey me—and I leave you. I dump you. No matter where we are. *Understand?*"

Her jaw tightened. "I just wanted to—"

"I don't care what you wanted. Do not compromise me like that ever again. My job is to keep you alive and I intend to deliver."

"Dammit, Luke, this may be your job, but it's my *life.*"

"If the Triad gets you, Jessica, you aren't going to have a life."

"I'm not going to have one after tomorrow, anyway," she retorted. "Not *my* life. I have fought for my entire existence to be acknowledged, can you understand this, Luke? I had to hack my way out of borderline poverty with a single mother who worked three jobs just to get me an education and keep a roof over our heads. You know what?" Her eyes burned with emotion. "I want what I have earned. I want justice. I do *not* want to hide like this—" Her voice caught. "You told me not to think like a victim, Luke—well I'm not. I refuse to be pushed under the goddamn carpet again. I refuse to run. Don't you see?"

He glowered at her, a muscle thumping angrily in his neck.

"You know what? Just dump me if you want. Right here. I didn't ask to be your…assignment." She opened the door, swung her legs out.

"Where do you think you're going?" he asked coolly.

"Perhaps I'll stay right here, in the mountains. Seems like a nice town." She got out.

"They'll find you, Jess."

"I don't really care, Luke. It's not like I have a life worth keeping."

She slammed the door in his face and stomped off in the snow.

Luke shut his eyes momentarily. Fine. Let her go. Let her walk right out of his life. He'd had it with Jacques and the FDS anyway. They were in breach of his contract—he was under no obligation to fulfill this mission. Let the damn woman go.

Jessica made her way steadily toward the ski lifts, her slight frame pushing through the crowds, snow settling on her long dark hair like wedding rice. Raw instinct surged through Luke. Even as his brain screamed to let her go, he just couldn't leave her.

This had become more than a delivery job. He wanted to help this woman. And in doing so, a part of Luke knew instinctively he would be helping himself.

If he allowed her to get hurt, it would be the end of him.

He swore violently, thrust open the door and marched after her.

Luke snagged Jessica's arm and whirled her round, the harsh words on his tongue dying instantly as he saw her cheeks were wet with streaming tears. He cursed to himself.

"Jess," he said softly. "You're being ridiculous."

She stood silent, glowering at him through her tears, and he could feel her shaking.

"Come back to the car with me, Jess. You're still in shock. You've been through a lot and you're going through a post-traumatic reaction. It's natural," he said cupping her face gently, vaguely aware that his body was thudding with more adrenaline than it did on a combat mission.

She sniffed and wiped her nose angrily.

"Come back to the car, please? We…can talk about this." Christ, now he was negotiating. Pleading. He could give her a wad of cash, tell her to hole up in a hotel for the night, inform the CIA of her location. And he'd be free. He could go back to being himself. He had choice here.

Or did he?

A part of Luke knew he hadn't really had a choice since he laid hands on her in Gastown. One touch and she'd sucked him right into her world.

She lifted her whisky eyes slowly, looking right into his soul. "Will you promise me one thing, Luke?"

"What?"

"That you will go and visit my mother, let her know I'm alive, but can never make contact again."

His heart wrenched. "Jess—"

"Promise me."

He began to breathe hard. He couldn't do it. He could not make that promise. He placed his hands on her shoulders. "Jess, listen to me. The first people the Dragon Heads will be watching in an effort to find you will be your family. If I go anywhere near your mother, it will put her in jeopardy."

The pain in her eyes was unbearable.

Luke felt vaguely nauseous. He ached to tell her something different. Instead he drew her closer, wrapped his arms tight around her, just held her for a moment, compassion mushrooming from somewhere deep inside him, overwhelming him. "She means a lot to you, doesn't she?"

She nodded against his chest and Luke felt his eyes burn.

"Jessica, come back to the car and ID those photos for me," he said softly against her hair. Just maybe if he could learn why those men were in Vancouver, he could find her a way out of this.

She pulled back. "They came out?"

He nodded.

She gave a tremulous little smile and smudged the tears from her eyes.

He hooked his arm around her shoulders and they walked back to the car, their bodies close, a new and uneasy partnership between them, an unknown and dangerous road ahead.

Dangerous in too many ways to count.

* * *

The first of four images filled Luke's laptop monitor. The photos, taken with a powerful telephoto lens, were of men inside a limousine. The door of the luxury vehicle was being held open and the faces of two men talking inside were clear. The face of a third man was partially obscured by shadow.

"These are brilliant, Jess." He couldn't help admiring her work.

"The ones on the first roll were better," she said. "The limo door was open more. But the Triad took those."

"What we have here is enough. The faces are clear, apart from that third guy," said Luke. "Any idea who he is?"

She shook her head. "No."

Luke opened the remaining files, the photos he'd taken at the firebombing scene. As the images filled his monitor he saw he'd clearly captured the license plates, along with several faces that could be digitally enhanced for possible identification. The cops were going to like this when he finally handed them over. Luke committed the plates to memory.

"Not so bad yourself, cowboy," she said, studying his photographs over his shoulder.

He crooked a brow. *"Cowboy?"*

A glint of mischief brightened her eyes. "I have this mental image of you on a horse in the outback with a cowboy-style bush hat."

He peered at her. "You are kidding me, right?"

She smiled. "Okay—I saw the photo on your fridge. It was the only one in your house that had people in it. I figured one of the guys on the horses was you. Who were the other two?"

"My brothers."

Her mouth opened in surprise. "As in...*siblings?*"

"Yeah."

She gave a small laugh. "I...I just..."

"Just what?"

"I know it's dumb, but I just don't see you as belonging to family."

He turned away and stared blankly at the monitor, the im-

plication in her words driving much deeper than he should
allow them.

"I'm from Perth," he said suddenly, still staring at his
monitor. "I was born there, but lived in Sydney mostly. And
Brisbane. Moved around a lot with the job." He clicked open
another file. "Did close protection work with the Australian
Secret Service and federal police before joining the FDS." He
didn't have to tell her this. He didn't know why he had.

Maybe he felt he owed her something.

Hell no, she owed him. *She* was the one who got his house
bombed and had killed his employment prospects in Vancouver.
She was the one making him feel things he thought he would
never again.

"Do you see your brothers often?" she asked.

He should not have had that photo on display. It was the one
little link he hadn't managed to chuck with the rest of his past,
the one weakness he'd allowed himself. He wasn't sure why
he'd been unable to toss it. Perhaps he'd wanted some kind of
safety line, just in case he chose to go back.

Jessica wouldn't have seen it if he hadn't been forced to
take her into his home in the first place. He never took anyone
there. "No," he said quietly. "I don't see them. Haven't been
back in years."

"How many years?"

"Three."

The first year after his wife's death had been spent in an alcoholic haze of self-loathing. When he realized he wasn't going
to die and that he couldn't muster the balls to take his own life,
he'd cleaned up, shipped out of the country and never looked
back. Instead, he went to Africa to join the FDS.

He wasn't going to tell her about that part.

He clicked onto the close-up of the men's faces in ,he limo
and cleared his throat. "Who's who in this photo?"

She hesitated, studying his face, before turning her attention
back to the computer. "That man on the left is Xiang-Li. I'll
never forget his face. This guy on the right is The Chemist."

"I'm impressed you stuck around long enough to get such good shots."

"I was torn between fleeing and finally having proof."

Proof that would now force her into witness protection, instead of helping her reclaim her life—the very reason she'd found the courage to stand her ground and take these photos in the first place. "And you went straight to the RCMP?"

"I was on the bus, going home to develop the film, but I started to get really nervous, and I wasn't sure how long they'd be in Chinatown. That's when I went to the RCMP."

"As opposed to the Vancouver cops?"

"Well, yes, they're federal."

He pursed his lips, nodded. She'd been thinking every step of the way. A logical mind under fear, in spite of what she'd endured at the hands of these very men. This was not a woman of unsound mind. Not at all.

"The RCMP told me to come back once I'd developed the prints, but of course I never got the chance to do that. My apartment was broken into that night."

"What still puzzles me Jess, is how the Dragon Heads got the information that you had these photos in the first place. Do you think someone saw you taking them and followed you from Chinatown?"

"No, I don't. And if they were following me, why wait for me to go to the cops and develop the film?"

Luke nodded. "You're right. Somehow the information was leaked from the RCMP to the Triad. Did you tell the cops you shot more than one roll?"

"Yes, I did."

He inhaled deeply, a cold and dark foreboding settling in his belly. "The only feasible explanation for this is that the Dragon Heads have an informant in the federal police force, but there's something much deeper, more sinister going on here, Jess."

She studied him in silence, her face pale.

"I'll send these to Sauvage," Luke said as he closed the files. "His techs can run biometrics data against The Chemist's profile." He shot her a wry grin. "He'll be mad as hell when he sees this."

"But he'll do it?" she asked.

"Sauvage owes me. And the intelligence will be valuable to the FDS. It's why I was stationed here in the first place. It'll take him all of one second to deal with his frustration before he runs with those images," Luke said as he attached the photos to his e-mail, firing off the information using an encrypted system.

"What about the CIA? Won't they have a problem with the pictures getting out?"

"Give them these negatives," he said handing her the envelope. "They don't need to know I've seen the images or forwarded them to the FDS."

The light left her eyes as she took the negatives from him and he knew she was thinking about tomorrow.

He hooked a knuckle under her chin. "Hey, one step at a time, Jess. Let's see what Jacques's men dig up."

She leaned forward suddenly, kissed him lightly on the mouth, a feather of sensation that shimmered like a hot electrical current right to his toes.

"Thank you," she whispered, her body so close he couldn't breathe. "I know you didn't have to do this, Luke. And I appreciate the risk you're taking." Her almond eyes filled with emotion. "I really do."

Luke had to fight the compulsion to press his mouth down hard on hers as the memory of their first searing kiss sent erotic thoughts rippling too close to the surface for comfort.

A charged silence consumed the car. Luke inhaled deeply and turned on the ignition. A few more hours—he just had to hang in a few more hours. And then she would be out of his life.

I don't want to go into witness protection...I don't want to live like that.

Her words snaked through his mind as he drove off. He tried not to think about them.

Or how she made him feel.

Or what he was going to do about it if he didn't get her into CIA hands real soon.

Chapter 7

It was growing dark when they drove into the tiny farming community of Pemberton. Tattered curtains of cloud raked through a gunmetal sky, opening momentarily to allow a shaft of pale light to hit Mount Currie. It was God's country, thought Jessica—breathtaking. She stared up at the avalanche chutes that plunged down the massive north face of the mountain. "That's the peak in your photograph, isn't it?" she said, feeling awed by the sheer size of it. "The one in your living room."

He nodded.

"You come up here often?"

"I do. You can reach the Pemberton Ice Cap from here. Awesome terrain."

"You go alone?"

"Always."

"Isn't that risky?"

"Wouldn't be a challenge if it wasn't."

"You like beating yourself up, don't you, Luke? What is it— the thrill? Tempting death? Self-flagellation?"

He glanced sideways at her. "Spending time in a mental institution turned you into an analyst, did it, Jess?"

A chill washed over her. "I suppose I deserved that."

He shrugged. "Sorry," he said after a while. "I didn't mean it that way."

The town centre had a distinct Western feel, right down to the old facade on the hotel, the log hitching posts and the locals from the nearby Mount Currie reserve wearing wide cowboy hats.

Luke pulled into the hotel parking lot. "Wait here."

She nodded, noting something subtle had shifted in him. He seemed unsure of where he was with her.

She didn't know herself.

He held her gaze a moment before getting out of the car, as if wanting to say something. Wanting to touch her. Jessica's pulse quickened and she swallowed at what she saw in his gray eyes. And then he was gone, the door slamming shut behind him as he strode toward the hotel entrance.

Clouds lowered the sky and the wind began to whip again, tiny flakes of snow brushing against the windshield as the temperature plummeted. Luke got back into the car with a sudden whoosh of cold air. He sat silent for a moment.

"The only room they have left is a single," he said avoiding her eyes.

"As in one bed?"

"Yep. Several groups of snowmobilers have come off the ice cap because of the coming storm and are holing up in the valley for the night." He turned slowly and met her eyes. "Can you handle sharing a bed?"

Butterflies flickered through Jessica's stomach at the thought of sleeping with Luke and she felt her cheeks warm. "Sure." She was anything but.

"Okay. Then let's go get something to eat."

Jessica exhaled slowly, a hot and anxious sensation quivering deep in her stomach as he drove. If she didn't know better, she'd think it was nervous anticipation. Unbidden images of

Luke Stone—naked and ripped—began to fill her mind and warmth pooled low in her belly.

She closed her eyes, wondering what she would do if he touched her, or if he was too controlled to act on the dark desire she'd seen lurking in his eyes.

Luke stepped out of the Dead Hang Saloon and called Jacques while Jessica waited for their order at a log table inside the tiny pub. A few snowmobiles were parked out front and a couple more rested on the sled rigs of big trucks. Two huskies with ice-blue eyes waited patiently under the warm lights of the rustic, snow-covered porch.

The highway south had been shut due to heavy snowfall and several collisions, and it would likely stay that way most of the night, judging by the way the weather was socking in. Luke felt fairly secure. It meant this already-isolated community was cut off for the night, and this was the kind of rugged place you stuck out if you didn't belong. A Dragon Heads member would be seen a mile off—if he could even get this far.

"The one man in the photographs is definitely Xiang-Li," Jacques Sauvage said, his tone cool. He was clearly irritated Luke had stepped beyond the bounds of the mission by developing the film, but Luke knew Jacques would have done it himself.

So would half the men he hired. Jacques Sauvage employed them precisely because they were renegades. And even though his boss was showing his displeasure, Luke could tell he was ultimately pleased to have the information.

"Xiang-Li is a wanted criminal in several countries," said Jacques. "But the Chinese have sheltered him from prosecution ostensibly because of Xiang's political stance against an independent Taiwan. Under Xiang, the Dragon Heads now control organized crime in Taiwan and our recent intelligence from that region shows the Triad is pushing a markedly pro-mainland agenda. Xiang is an advocate of China's long-standing vow to recover the self-ruled island by force if necessary."

"So these guys are definitely moving into a political arena?"

"It looks that way."

That would explain the CIA interest, thought Luke. The United States had long been Taiwan's main ally and Washington had promised to defend the island against Chinese military attack.

"We don't yet have a match on The Chemist," said Jacques, "but our techs are running some experimental biometrics technology against global databases, including our own. If his photo is on record anywhere, we *will* find it."

"What about the third man, the one in shadow—were you able to enhance that image?"

Jacques hesitated and Luke could tell he would rather hold back the next bit of information. "That man," said Jacques quietly, "is Ben Woo—personal assistant to the Chinese deputy consul-general in San Francisco."

Luke's pulse quickened. "Are you *sure?*"

"Very."

His thoughts raced. "That means Chan's photos connect the Dragon Heads and their assassin directly to a Chinese government employee."

"Yes."

"*That's* why the CIA wants those photographs. Something is going down here in the Pacific Northwest, maybe an assassination."

Jacques tone was firm. "It's CIA business, Stone. Get Chan on that chopper tomorrow, and get out of the country. I want you back here on São Diogo for a debriefing before the week is out, *comprends?*"

"Yeah, yeah. I'll be there."

But he wasn't so sure he would. Jessica Chan had landed herself bang in the middle of some major global intrigue and Luke was worried she was going to end up a pawn. Again.

And it would break her.

He wasn't sure what he could do about that—his only choice at the moment was to hand her over.

He began to pace through the snow, making sure he was well

out of earshot. "Xiang must have entered Canada using a false passport," he said quietly.

"We're accessing passenger manifests from Vancouver International to see if we can pick up what ID he's using. If no red flags are raised, we'll expand the search."

Luke felt a wry smile tug at his lips. So the FDS *was* running with this. He knew they'd take the bait, even if only to bolster their own intelligence databases.

"Where will you be tonight?" asked Jacques.

"We're in Pemberton. We'll be at the only hotel here."

"Stone—" Jacques hesitated. "There is something else I must tell you...for information purposes only."

Luke went cold at the tone in Jacques's voice. "What?"

"The Circle K Triad in Australia has just been cannibalized by the Dragon Heads. The top three Circle K bosses were assassinated two days ago. It appears Dragon Heads moles have been working from within the Circle K syndicate for several years to make this happen." He paused. "It turns out one of those moles was among the Circle K men you killed in the Australian shootout four years ago, when you were protecting the minister."

The news shattered like a shell through Luke's chest. He couldn't breathe. His hands tightened on the phone, and his world narrowed instantly. The Circle K was the Triad that had killed his wife. His child. Because of that shootout.

"Stone?"

He had to force sound through his throat. "Yeah. I'm here."

"The information is for your personal purposes only."

"That's why you want me out of the country, isn't it?" Luke said. "The Dragon Heads are going to come after me regardless of Jessica Chan. They've been waiting until now to do it. Any earlier and they might have blown their Australian takeover operation."

"It's possible and that's why I'm telling you, so that you can take precautions."

Luke swore as he dragged his hand over his snow-covered hair. If it wasn't for this gig, he might have remained anonymous. But now that his cover had been blown, he was going to be hunted down across the globe, no matter where he went. Just like Jessica.

Her enemy had just become his.

"Stone, just get your package onto that helo, and we'll work on a new identity for you here in São Diogo."

Her name is Jessica—she's a person, not a goddamn package.

"Affirmative," Luke said through clenched teeth. He hung up and stomped back through the snow to the saloon.

The Circle K Triad had already exacted their revenge on him for killing several members in a shootout while he was protecting a top Australian politician bent on eradicating organized crime. They'd punished Luke by torturing and killing his pregnant wife.

Now because a Dragon Heads mole had been among the men Luke had shot, it appeared he had to pay twice.

He'd die before he let those guys get their hands on Jessica. If the Dragon Heads got her now, they weren't just going to kill her. They would make her suffer—torture her in the most horrible way. Like they had his wife. And they'd do it to punish *him.*

Then they would kill her.

Luke was suddenly going head-to-head with an intimately familiar and lethal foe. One that had grown much more powerful. Well, he'd grown more dangerous, too—he had nothing more to lose.

But as Luke pushed open the saloon door and saw Jessica sitting at the table by the fire, he knew he was wrong. He did have something to lose.

She smiled and waved at him from across the crowded room and Luke's heart torqued.

This mission could not have become more intimately personal. And in this moment, he knew he had to get her on that chopper tomorrow—because he couldn't keep her safe. Not on his own. Not with this kind of threat.

But right now he just had to get her through the night.

Once she was safely in CIA hands, he'd deal with his nemesis. On his own terms.

* * *

"Feels like my last supper," Jessica said with a smile as Luke joined her at the rough-hewn table near the fire.

"What do you mean?" he said, angling himself so he had a keen view of the door.

She frowned. His energy has shifted. He had that cold, hard edge back. A distance in his eyes. "You know exactly what I mean, Luke," she said picking up her sandwich. "I get on that chopper tomorrow and I cease to exist."

He said nothing as a server brought their drinks. She placed a bottle of beer in front of Jessica and an iced tea in front of Luke.

Jessica reached for her beer. "You not going to join me with a beer?"

He shook his head.

"Do you ever lighten up, Luke Stone?"

His eyes narrowed suddenly. "I lighten up and you die, Jessica."

"Sorry I asked," she muttered.

"I happen to like iced tea," he said as a guy in a loggers shirt across the small room raised two fingers in greeting at Luke. He tipped his head in response.

"You're not worried about being recognized?" she asked, biting into her sandwich, noting he hadn't yet touched his food.

"No. I come here often enough that I don't stand out, but they don't know who I am. They don't know my name."

"You use an alias everywhere you go?"

He nodded, absorbed in some thought as his eyes panned the room. His sudden detachment made Jessica uncomfortable.

She swallowed her food. "So there's no way these people here will link you to news of a boathouse explosion on Granville Island?"

His eyes flashed suddenly back to hers. "You just don't stop with the questions, do you?" There was an edge of anger in his tone.

Her mouth flattened. Something had really changed in him since he made that call. "What happened outside, Luke?"

"Nothing for you to worry about."

Jessica pushed her plate to the side. She no longer felt hungry. All she knew was that she never wanted to be like Luke Stone. He was a distant cipher, mingling with people who recognized him by sight, but who never knew his name, where he lived. Who he really was.

But that's exactly what will happen to me once I get on that chopper tomorrow.

The thought made her nauseous.

"It's like being the walking dead," she muttered as she took a sip of her beer.

"Pardon?"

She leaned forward over the table, lowering her voice as she held his eyes. "You walk like a ghost among these people, Luke. They think you're one of them but you're not. They know absolutely nothing about you. You may be alive and breathing but you're totally cut off from *living*."

Something darkened dangerously in his features, but Jessica didn't back off. "What does that do to a person over the long term, Luke? Why would you even want it? Why would it be a choice?"

The barbed look in his eyes sharpened.

She set her bottle down carefully on the wooden table, watching the condensation connect with the wood, then lifted her eyes to his. "Why do you do it, Luke?" she asked softly. "This work can't be fun."

"It's not about fun," he said, reaching for his sandwich.

"Right. It's about lies, about deception."

He said nothing, bit into his sandwich, the look on his face warning her to stop, but she couldn't.

While he might be content in his isolation, she wasn't. Jessica needed to connect with people. Especially now. Especially *him*. Truth be told, she was afraid—of being cut off from her own identity forever, starting tomorrow. It fed a strange recklessness in her. She leaned closer, meeting his gaze steadily. "So why *do* you do this, Luke? What made you leave Australia?"

His eyes locked fast onto hers, his neck muscles cording.

A singer began to strum his guitar in the corner, an old country song.

The fire crackled next to their table, the warmth of the small pub shielding them against the winter wilderness outside as the snow came down harder and the wind began to rattle frozen twigs against the window panes.

He took a swig of his tea, not breaking eye contact. "Jess," he said finally, darkly, almost inaudibly. "You're going your way tomorrow and I'm going mine. Let's just keep things simple until then."

"Simple?"

"Yeah. Simple."

She snorted. "There's nothing simple here, Luke. Like you said, I'm going away tomorrow, so why don't you humor me. Tell me—" she leaned even closer to him, defiantly searching for a way to tap into him, to reconnect, maybe even to hold on to him for a while longer, even though she had a sense she'd lost whatever small bond they shared. He'd decided to cut her out. "What happened in Australia, Luke?"

His mouth grew tight. She watched his lips, knowing exactly what they could do to her body, wondering if she could entice him to put them against hers again. Just one more time. A warmth began to unfurl dangerously low in her belly and she saw heat darken his eyes.

The music swelled louder. So did voices and the clatter of plates and cutlery. More people arrived, dusting snow off their jackets and stomping boots at the door. But she watched only him, steadily, meeting the predatory intensity in his gaze, finding his features, his masculine presence, more compelling by the second.

"It was a woman, wasn't it?" she said, her voice turning husky. "That's why you left."

Something snapped in him. So sharp and so visceral she felt a physical jolt.

He got up. "We should go."

She grabbed his wrist. "No," she said. She had a driving need to know this one thing about her savior before he disappeared from her life forever.

He glowered at her hand gripping his wrist, then raised his eyes, slowly sweeping the length of her arm, the contours of her body, the line of her neck, before his gaze settled on hers. The untamed look in them curled something hot and deep and primitive in her.

He sank very slowly back down to the bench, eyes pinning her. Nerves trembled low in her belly. "You know everything about me, Luke," she whispered. "Is it so wrong for me to be interested in you?"

Something hot and sexual flickered in his eyes and Jessica felt her mouth go dry.

"Your interest in me," he said, his voice rough, "could get us both hurt."

"I'm not going to be around long enough for that to happen, Luke," she said, tentatively feathering the back of his hand lightly with her fingertips as she watched his eyes.

He swallowed. "Believe me, Jessica, I'm not a man you want to be interested in." He lowered his gaze to stare at her hand touching his, then he lifted those gray eyes slowly, fixing them on her mouth, and she saw raw lust in his features. "Why are you doing this?" His voice was gravelly, thick.

She swallowed a ball of sadness that rose suddenly in her throat. She felt so very alone. "I just need to connect, Luke," she said softly. "I…it's who I am. Maybe I'm scared. I don't know what will happen to me after tomorrow."

He was silent for an incredibly long time, his eyes probing hers. The sounds of the restaurant muted into the distance as they became an island, locked into something shared only by them.

"I had a wife once, Jessica," he said very quietly. "She was seven months pregnant. My job was to protect people. But I couldn't protect her and the baby."

Blood drained from her head. The music and convivial laughter suddenly seemed loud.

"Luke, I…I am so sorry. I…what happened?"

"She was executed," he said simply, staring at her hand resting on his. "Our baby was cut from her belly while she was kept alive long enough to see him for the first time." He lifted his eyes. "Long enough for her to watch our unborn child die."

Jessica's stomach lurched. "*Who did this?*" she whispered.

"A triad in Australia that is now controlled by the Dragon Heads. As of two days ago." He leaned forward. "I told you, Jess, I'm *intimately* familiar with the workings of triads and tongs. I know how they hunt people down, how they make them pay." He paused, watching her face. "They made me pay. By murdering my family."

Jessica couldn't talk. The range of raw emotions etched into his features was like nothing she'd ever seen. It ripped at her very soul.

"Why did you have to pay?" Her words came out hoarse.

"I killed some of their men."

"*Why?*"

He exhaled heavily as he rubbed the back of his neck. "I was on close-protection detail for a high-profile Australian politician whose campaign against organized crime had made him a target. In saving his life, I was forced to take the lives of several key triad members."

"So they came after you?" She thought of the scars on his back.

"They wanted information, the name of an informant inside their operation working for Australian federal law enforcement."

"And you didn't tell them."

"It wasn't mine to tell."

"So they went for your family—they didn't kill you."

He looked at her for a long time.

"They did kill me, Jess," he said quietly.

Then he got up and walked out, leaving her alone at the table.

Jessica closed her eyes and pressed her palms flat against the table. She inhaled deeply, thinking of the terrible scars on his back. Of how she'd called him the walking dead. Remorse swallowed her. It was exactly what he was—a ghost. It was the same aloneness she'd seen in his photographs—not another human in sight, not even a footprint in the snow.

They must have tortured him first. Then when he hadn't given them what they wanted, they'd found another way to go at him. A way to hurt him beyond death. And it had killed his soul.

She jerked to her feet, ran out into the dark night, pulling on her down jacket as she went. He stood by his SUV, staring into the swirling snow.

Jessica stilled.

She ached to rush right up to him, wrap her arms around him, comfort him. Apologize. At the same time she had a desperate need to know more—how many years he'd been married, how long ago this had happened.

She took a tentative step toward him. Stopped again. She understood this man now, as best one could. Because in some ways, she'd been there. She'd had everything taken from her, too.

And come tomorrow, she'd be forced to be as much a cipher in this world as he. A walking ghost.

She didn't want to be like that.

It wasn't fair that he still suffered like this. There *had* to be a better way. For *both* of them.

She went up, touched his arm. "Luke?"

He glanced down at her. "We should call it a night, Jess." His voice was different. Wounded. Yet still so powerfully male it made her heart ache.

She nodded. It had been a long day.

Much too long.

Luke lay on his back in their ground-floor room, arms behind his head as he stared up into blackness, listening to the thudding music coming from the hotel bar where snowmobilers were testing their mettle on a mechanical bull.

The room was too hot, the thermostat broken. Jessica lay beside him, freshly showered, wearing her panties and his oversize T-shirt. No bra. He couldn't help but notice.

The mattress didn't help matters. It dipped in the middle so he had to fight rolling into her and feeling her smooth, honey-toned skin against his. He swallowed against the rough dryness in his throat. There was no denying his sexual desire for this incredible woman lying so close to him. A woman who'd found a way right into his soul.

He wondered how she'd respond if he rolled over and touched her—if she'd soften against him, open her legs for him. He'd tasted her own hunger for him in her kiss. He'd seen it in her eyes tonight. And the lingering memory of her lips against his, the feel of her tongue slick in his mouth, just made his arousal throb hotter and harder between his thighs.

He cursed to himself.

This was pure torture.

This woman was tearing at the iron control that had kept him together over these past three years.

She'd made him need her in the most visceral, aching way. Luke would have made a move on her earlier this evening, but he sensed her need was driven by desperate loneliness and fear. He couldn't take advantage of that.

He also knew instinctively that if he slept with her, he'd lose any last shred of control over himself. And he'd put her in deeper danger.

He closed his eyes, trying to focus on the bar sounds and the noises on the floor above them until the night eventually fell silent around 2:00 a.m., the kind of muffled, heavy silence that came with winter snow.

And with the eerie quiet came an even deeper awareness of Jessica's proximity. Luke gritted his teeth, sat up abruptly and swung his legs over the bed.

That's when he heard it.

A faint sound outside. A soft crunch on snow.

His chest snapped tight. He quickly pulled on his pants and reached for his gun belt. Sliding his Sig from the holster, he moved like a shadow to the window.

Luke raised the blinds infinitesimally with the backs of his fingers.

Three figures moved like black ghosts through the snow toward the hotel entrance.

His pulse accelerated.

He'd never have heard them if he'd been asleep instead of obsessing over Jessica. He squinted into the dim light, tracking the men's prints back through heavy snow to two dark SUVs parked in shadow. He could just make out the first three characters on one of the plates.

It was the same as the one in his photograph.

"Jessica!" he hissed.

She woke almost instantly. "What...what is it?"

"Take the knife from the sheath next to the bed and go hide behind the door. No matter what happens, stay out of sight."

To her credit, she didn't question him.

She scrambled across the covers, grabbed the knife, rolled out of bed and positioned herself behind the door in bare feet and T-shirt, blade glinting in the dark.

Luke moved back from the window and lowered himself behind the bed. He carefully aimed the barrel of his 9 mm toward the door, finger gentle on the trigger as he reached for his boots, making a mental note of where Jessica's clothes were folded in a neat pile on a chair near his backpack and computer.

"Expect three," he whispered across the room. "I'll take at least the first two by surprise, but, Jess—"

"What?" she hissed in the dark.

"Use the knife if you have to. Fight like your life depends on it."

Because it did.

Chapter 8

Jessica clutched the knife as she pressed back against the wall, her mouth dry as dust. Sweat beaded along her forehead and dampened her chest, her stomach tightening as the sickening images of Stephanie's stabbing rolled through her head.

She flicked a desperate glance at Luke for reassurance.

He'd put his jeans and boots on, but his powerful chest was bare, muscles gleaming in the faint light seeping through the blinds as he aimed his pistol at the door. He was so solid, just the sight of him grounded her.

Then she heard something out in the corridor.

With a massive crash, the door splintered open and smacked back against the wall, just missing her. Jessica swallowed a scream as three men burst into the room.

Luke fired three shots in rapid succession. The men returned fire. Disoriented by the dark and the surprise ambush, their shots went wild. Luke fired another round.

One man slumped to the floor with a grunt. Another staggered sideways against the wall, holding his neck, shouting in

Chinese for backup, before sliding slowly down, tracking a trail of glistening blood over white paint as he went. The third man lay unmoving on the carpet.

Luke lurched toward the window, shooting through the glass at someone outside. Shards blew outward as the entire pane shattered down. He grabbed his jacket, wrapped it once around his fist, and knocked out jagged bits of glass that remained.

The man on the floor behind him lifted his head and began dragging himself slowly along the carpet leaving a river of blood in his wake. Jessica's stomach churned as she watched the man use the bed to pull himself up. He raised his gun, aimed the barrel at Luke's back.

Luke hadn't seen him.

Jessica had to do it. Now. She raised the knife high over her head, and surged forward with a high-pitched scream, plunging the tip down into the man's back. She felt blade hit bone, then sink with a sickening soft resistance through flesh all the way to the hilt. Bile lurched into her throat. She gritted her teeth, yanked out the blade, and stabbed it into flesh again. The man went rigid, then splayed forward onto the bed, where he twitched and then lay motionless, a soft gurgling sound coming from his lungs.

Tears began to spill furiously down Jessica's cheeks.

"Get the knife out!" Luke yelled as he grabbed his pack.

She squeezed her eyes shut, grasped the hilt, now slippery and warm with blood, and yanked it. The blade slicked out with a horrible little wet sound and glistened in her hands. Jessica couldn't move. She was going to faint.

On the edge of her fading consciousness she heard more shooting, a car engine, people screaming upstairs. The thudding of footsteps down the hall.

Luke snagged her arm, hauled her over to the window, and thrust her bundle of clothes and parka into her hands. "Take these! Watch for glass!" Jessica was vaguely aware of Luke forcing her out over the windowsill, of falling into snow. He seized her arm, jerked her to her feet, and dragged her, barelegged, through several feet of fresh powder. She didn't register the cold. She was only distantly aware of the driving wind and sharp needles of ice stinging her skin. Of more screaming, yelling.

He bundled her into his SUV, yelling at her to buckle up as he tossed his pack into the back, climbed in, slammed the door and floored the gas. Their tires spun, and churning through several feet of snow, they fishtailed wildly out of the parking lot.

Luke drove blindly along a narrow farm road, full speed into the teeth of the mounting blizzard. He opened his window, steering with one hand as he tried to knock snow off the windshield with the other.

Only when he was certain he could hear no sirens above the howl of the wind did he ease off on the gas a little, concentrating on just staying on the road. Conditions were borderline whiteout, snowdrifts already several feet deep and accumulating fast.

He knew there were two RCMP members stationed in Pemberton, but by the time they reached the hotel and called for backup from Whistler, their tire tracks would be long gone. Air pursuit would also be impossible.

Tonight the blizzard was their friend.

A dense hush descended over the wilderness as they left farmland, entering a heavy forest of ghostly white trees that shielded them from the wind. Luke slowed even more and was finally able to steal a glance at Jessica.

She was shivering, still clutching the bloody knife tightly in her hands, eyes glassy with shock, her legs and feet bare.

"Put the knife down, Jess," he said, as he cranked up the heat.

She didn't respond.

"Jess, I said put the knife on the floor. Get some clothes on. Now."

She turned a taut, pale face to him. "I killed him."

"You did what you had to do, Jess."

"I…I've never killed anyone."

Luke wanted to tell her you got used to the killing. But the truth was, you didn't. You just learned how to hide from the emotion, cut it off, intellectualize. Luke was good at hiding, blotting emotion out. He was realizing this more and more since he'd met Jess.

"They killed Stephanie. Remember that. They killed Giles. And they would have killed us, too."

"I didn't know I *could* kill a man," she said in a small voice, staring at the bloody blade.

"We're human, Jess," he said gently. "We're not built to want to die. You don't think when it goes down to the wire like that." He paused. "You did good. You saved my ass back there. Thank you."

She said nothing.

"Now please, put the knife on the floor."

"Where are we going?"

"First get your pants and jacket on, and your boots. It's six degrees out there."

Luke returned his concentration to the road. The drifts were getting deeper, his headlights weak little halos being reflected back at him by driving whiteness. As soon as he could free his hands from the wheel, he'd tug his own shirt and jacket on. But right now, if he strayed too far to the right, they'd end up somewhere in the Lillooet river. He focused instead on hugging the fringe of ghostly conifers on their left, his nose up against the windshield as he searched for a turnoff.

He felt Jessica drape his jacket over his shoulders as he drove, and a jolt of affection almost overpowered him. He flicked his eyes over to her. "Thanks."

She smiled through the hollowness in her eyes. "You looked cold."

"I hadn't noticed," he said with a grim smile, pleased to see she was coming out of her shock.

"Do you know where we're going?"

He shook his head. "I think there's an old trapper's cabin somewhere out here used by the local gun club for hunting. If I can find the deactivated logging road that leads off this one, it should take us there. We can hole up there for a few hours until daybreak. Hopefully the weather will clear and the CIA can get their chopper in."

Luke broke the padlock and creaked open the wooden door, directing his flashlight into the gloom. Wind whistled eerily through the old slats of an adjacent woodshed, but inside the rustic abode was protected and dry.

The trail leading to the cabin had proved impassable by four-wheel drive, and they'd had to hike in through thigh-deep drifts. Jessica was deathly cold, toes and fingers completely numb. Her body wasn't cooperating with her brain and Luke recognized the early signs of hypothermia on top of her shock.

He moved fast, lighting a candle and smashing open a supply cupboard. He grabbed blankets, spare clothes. "Here, put this on, all of it," he commanded as he thrust an oversize flannel shirt, giant T-shirt, wool hat, socks and long johns at her. He lit a kerosene lamp, and handed her the lighter. "Take this," he barked. "When you're dressed, start the gas on this stove." He grabbed her by the shoulders. "Jess? Are you listening to me? Can you do this?"

She gritted her teeth and nodded between violent shivers.

"Good. Keep moving. I'm going outside to get wood."

Jessica had the stove going and a pot of water steaming by the time Luke blew back into the cabin with a blast of frigid air and swirling flakes. He kicked the door shut behind him and clattered the bundle of wood to the floor.

Soon the crackling of fire and the comforting scent of pine resin and wood smoke filled the cabin with warmth, and the water on the gas stove was rolling to a boil.

Luke quickly made soup from packets he'd found in the supply cupboard, and he passed a steaming mugful to Jessica, who was huddled by the fire with a thick red tartan blanket over her shoulders. She winced as she tried to take the mug from him with frozen fingers.

He handed her a small flask of whiskey he'd discovered in

the food cache and she took a deep sip. Luke watched with relief as color flushed back into her cheeks.

"Thanks." Jessica smiled wanly as she offered the bottle to him.

He shook his head.

She cocked a brow quizzically. "You don't drink at all, do you?"

Luke studied her, searching for something in her eyes, wanting to trust her, to tell her everything. But he couldn't.

"It's okay, Luke. I…was just asking. I noticed."

He snatched the bottle from her, raised it to his lips to take a deep, angry swig, to feel that fast, familiar and numbing warmth course through him. He had a sudden urge to test the elixir again, to test *himself,* knowing just how good—and dangerous—it would feel in his mouth. Like her kiss.

Luke almost tilted the bottle, longing to feel the pleasure in his veins. But he stopped, unable to break his three-year stint of total abstinence.

Unable—unwilling—to test himself.

He was still afraid he would slide right back into mind-numbing drunkenness. He still feared losing control.

Frustrated, Luke lowered the bottle to his side and set it carefully in front of the fire, aware of her watching him intently.

He stared for a while into the flames, unable to meet her questioning eyes, memories creeping up on him. Painful ones. And with them came feelings. Powerful emotions he'd struggled so hard to keep at bay for so long.

Damn, he wouldn't mind dulling it all with a quick, hard swig.

He stole a quick look at Jessica. She'd stopped shivering now. She was wrapped in the blanket he'd given her, her feet tucked into oversize gray wool socks. The flames danced gold in her eyes as she gazed into the fire, lost in her own thoughts.

She was just as tempting and potentially intoxicating as the liquor, thought Luke, just as dangerous to him. Because he suddenly, desperately, wanted to hold on to her, have her, know everything about her, every little secret—what made her laugh, what made her love. He ached for the physical connection, for an affirmation of life in the face of the death they'd just managed to evade.

The sudden ferocity of his desires, the rawness of his need, disturbed him. It was all too overpowering. It was wrong. Pathetic.

He had to step away.

"We need more wood," he said as he lurched to his feet, grabbing a kerosene lamp.

He went outside into the bracing cold, welcoming it as he trudged through thigh-deep powder to the woodshed, and hung the lamp in the rafters.

He stared at the neat pile of split dry logs stacked high against the rear wall and began to chop more anyway. The physical task gave him a sense of purpose, a reason not to think about the liquor he'd almost allowed to pass his lips, the line he'd somehow crossed in wanting this woman.

The line he'd crossed within himself.

He swung the heavy ax and hacked at the wood under the eaves as snow swirled and dumped outside the door, just beyond the yellow glow of the lantern. He swung that ax until his muscles burned and sweat dripped from his body. He stripped off his shirt and he chopped some more, chest hot and naked in the winter night. Mindless action. Until he suddenly realized she'd followed him, was watching him from the flickering shadows just inside the door, wrapped in the red checkered blanket.

"You haven't let it go, have you, Luke?" she said quietly.

He stilled.

"You still blame yourself for what happened in Australia, don't you? That's why you punish yourself." Jessica took a step toward him. "You told me guilt was not the way to handle something like this, remember? You told me that I must stop thinking of myself as a victim, as if I somehow *deserved* this."

Jessica watched as he lowered the ax slowly to his side, copper light from the lantern gleaming on the perspiration that covered his skin, highlighting the raised veins in pumped forearms and biceps. He dragged his hand over his hair, looking slightly lost.

She went up to him, stood behind him, traced her fingertips ever so gently over the pale scars that traversed almost every inch of his back.

He stood dead still, as if afraid. This big, capable protector of hers was vulnerable at some point.

She'd found that point.

It endeared him to her terribly, awakening in Jessica a burning compulsion to comfort, to nurture, to hold him. It blunted the sharp edge of her own plight. It fed her with a sudden sense of purpose. She hadn't realized just how badly she'd needed to reach out and touch someone, to make a positive difference in someone else's life. It made her feel real in a very surreal world.

"Is this where they tortured you?" she said quietly, feeling the ridges under her fingertips.

He glanced at the white swirling madness of flakes outside that blocked them off from the world, and he closed his eyes.

"Luke?"

He whipped round suddenly and locked his eyes onto hers, chasing a sharp frisson of electrical energy over her skin.

"Yes." His voice was strange. "That's where they tortured me." His cool silver eyes bored into hers. "Physical pain, Jess, I can endure any amount of it. They discovered that. They saw that no amount of cutting me apart piece by piece was going to force me to give them what they wanted. The couldn't hurt me the way they *needed* to hurt me."

"So they went for something that would—your wife?" she said very softly.

His eyes narrowed and began to glisten with emotion in the reflected light of the kerosene lamp. "They took my family from me, Jess. They took my wife and my son."

Emotion ballooned in Jessica so fast it hurt. "What was her name?" she whispered.

"Rebecca." His features distorted with the pain as he said it. "They used an ancient method of execution on her—slow slicing, death by a thousand cuts. It ensured she'd live long enough for me to get to her…to hold her in my arms while she bled to death, but just not enough time to help her. They knew it would break me, Jess. It…" His voice cracked and he looked away, the muscle in his jaw quavering. "They knew making Rebecca die in my arms, making me *helpless,* was worse than dying myself."

He suddenly swung the ax up and violently cleft it into the stump, the impact shuddering though his muscular frame. He turned to face her squarely, his whole body humming with emotion and exertion, glistening with perspiration. "Well, they got what they wanted. They broke me."

She swallowed at the sheer intensity that vibrated from him. "Why didn't they kill you, Luke?"

"I told you, they did. Living itself became purgatory. Dying would have been a relief, yet it was something I could not bring myself to do."

"You wanted to kill yourself?" she said softly.

"Didn't have the balls." He paused, blew out air. "Or maybe I just felt I needed to keep living to keep punishing myself. Perhaps I should have given them the information they wanted. Rebecca would still be—"

Jessica placed two fingers over his lips, and shook her head. "No. You told me yourself there's no going back. You told me to deal with the road ahead, remember?"

He snagged her wrist, removing her hand from his mouth, his eyes narrowing. "If I could go back, I would choose to let her live. I would give the information."

"And how would she have felt then, Luke? Widowed and alone with her child, knowing you'd given up the name of an innocent man to save her?"

"That's just it, Jess. She didn't deserve that, either. My mistake," he said, "was loving someone. People like me have no right to get involved, not if they have any conscience."

Jessica looked deep into his haunted gray eyes as she placed her hand against the side of his face, feeling the rough stubble of his jaw under her palm. "You don't choose who you fall in love with, Luke."

"No, Jess, you don't," he said, holding her eyes. "But you do choose whether to act on it. Or not."

They both knew what he meant. They'd come to a turning point and the question of choice rose between them.

She answered by reaching for his hand that had wielded the ax and guiding it under her shirt, placing his roughened palm against the warmth of her bare breast, near her heart. His muscles were pumped from chopping, his calloused palm cold and rough against her tender skin. Her body responded instantly to the contrast, nipples bunching tight, heat spearing clean through to her belly.

She swallowed, holding his gray eyes steadily.

He stood stock-still, poised on the precarious cusp of decision, the hushed silence of the snowy woods growing complete. A dark and predatory hunger seeped into his eyes, making her pulse race and her mouth dry.

"Jess, I can't—" His voice was thick and hoarse.

"I'm leaving tomorrow, Luke," she whispered. "It's not a commitment. It's…" She didn't know what it was, but it was what she wanted. A connection. Visceral and real. "I just want you to hold me," she said softly. "I want to be with you."

Emotion surged into his eyes and his features tightened. He cupped her breast boldly, rasping her nipple with his roughened thumb as his eyes watched hers. Jessica's knees buckled and her vision swirled as she leaned into the overwhelming sensation, wanting it to take her, to swallow her completely.

He lowered his head, whispered against her ear. "Are you sure, Jessica?"

She nodded, unable to speak.

Urgency bit into his actions and he scooped her up, blanket and all. He carried her through the thigh-deep snow, toed the cabin door open, kicked it shut firmly behind him and lowered her to the floor in front of the fire.

He slid the blanket back off her shoulders, and began to unbutton her flannel shirt, his eyes locked steadfastly onto hers, his breathing hard, rapid.

Jessica's own breathing quickened. She wanted him badly. He was solid. Real. Safe. Something tough and physical in her out-of-control world of shadows and darkness.

Heat pooled in her center as he peeled back the soft flannel, sliding it tantalizingly down the length of her arms, trailing a shivering wake of sensitized nerves that tightened her nipples to such hard points they ached.

A low groan of approval emanated from inside him as he took in the sight of her aroused breasts, her flat stomach, the firelight flickering over her skin.

His lids lowered heavily and his eyes turned dark as thunderclouds.

He placed his hand flat on her belly, sliding his palm lower until his fingers reached the waistline of her oversize pants. Jessica's pulse raced dizzyingly as he began to undo her belt buckle, his eyes not once breaking contact with hers. She arched her pelvis up as he hooked his fingers inside and slid her clothes over her hips and down her legs, leaving her naked save for the small gold chain and pendant that rested at the hollow of her throat.

He sat back, chest gleaming in the firelight, appraising her with such brazen sexual intensity it made her cheeks flush and heat begin to pulse between her thighs.

Eyes still holding hers, he stood and unbuckled his gun belt, lowering his weapon to the rough wooden floor with a soft thud. He unzipped his pants as she watched, stepped out of them, his legs beautiful—massively muscular thighs, his arousal powerful. Jessica swallowed.

Even totally undressed this man did not appear naked. There was simply nothing vulnerable about his physique. If anything, the complete exposure of his body made him even more commanding, more potent. Luke Stone was not one of those men who needed cloth and trappings to give him the illusion of power.

What you saw was what you got—vital male strength, a walking human weapon. And the sensitivity she'd glimpsed lurking beneath the muscular surface of this man just made him even more beautiful to her.

So did his battle scars.

And the reason he'd earned them.

More than anything, Jessica was attracted by Luke's hidden capacity for love. This was clearly a one-woman guy who didn't fall easily, but when he did, he fell hard. And he fell forever.

As he lowered himself to the ground in front of her she wondered momentarily what it might be like to be on the receiving end of Luke Stone's undivided love. But her thoughts were blindsided by a hot thrill that chased through her chest and arrowed into her belly as he parted her legs slowly, positioning himself between them.

Jessica opened her legs wider as she reached up and drew his head down to hers, her lips finding his, her tongue seeking the warm slickness of his as she ran her other hand down his rock-hard abs toward his groin.

A low groan escaped from deep inside his chest as she cupped him between the thighs. She wrapped her fingers around his erection and pulled upward, beginning to massage him with rhythmic strokes. He began to breathe harder.

He was hot. Incredibly hard. She increased her rhythm.

It snapped his control.

Luke thrust his fingers into the hair at the nape of her neck and drew her more firmly to him as he deepened his kiss, groaning softly, using his knees to push her thighs open wider.

He slid his hand down her stomach and cupped her hard between her legs. Jessica went dizzy as she instinctively arched her pelvis, easing access. He slid his finger right up into her slick heat and Jessica moaned, opening even wider, desperate for full sensation, moving her hips in a way that drove his finger deeper into her.

He scored her lips with his teeth and slid another finger up into her, still kissing her as he moved, still massaging her deep inside, until he found such a sensitive and tingling spot that she gasped against his mouth as he touched it. She felt his lips smile against hers as he began to stroke, working in a way that made her arch wildly, tightening every muscle in her body until she wanted to scream for release. He stopped suddenly.

And she found herself gasping for breath as he positioned himself between her thighs. Using his fingers to open her folds wide, he placed the hot, smooth tip of his erection between her legs and with one solid, slick movement he thrust up into her, burying himself to the hilt.

Jessica arched her back, her vision swirling as her body tried to accommodate him.

He thrust again, moving harder and faster inside her, spreading her legs wider with his thighs as he did, his weight pinning her to the blanket on the floor, the hair of his chest deliciously rough against her breasts. She moved with him. Urgently. Rotating her hips, meeting his thrust, a searing heat rising to a sweet feverish pitch deep inside her.

Chapter 9

Luke threaded his fingers into her hair, tightening his grip, kissing her hard on the mouth as he raised her buttocks with his other hand, drawing her firmly against his pelvis as he thrust again, faster, going hotter and harder with each slick stroke, the sensation so achingly exquisite he thought he'd burst with sheer, blind bliss.

Jessica moaned against his mouth, her tongue tangling with his as she lifted and rotated her hips under him, driving him higher, hotter, her entire body growing damp against his.

Then he felt her go rigid under him and she began to tremble, nails cutting into his skin as she curved her back and held her breath. She shattered suddenly under him, crying out as her muscles began contracting around him in powerfully undulating waves.

His own orgasm welled from deep inside him. His vision turned scarlet and he couldn't hold back as an excruciatingly sweet heat speared through him. He bucked into her, release grabbing hold of his body in a shuddering, violent wave.

They lay like that, naked and sated, still coupled in front of the dying embers as if neither wanted to let go. Yet even as Luke stroked her hair, feeling her soft breasts against his chest, he knew he had to let her go. For her own survival.

And he'd probably never see her again.

Emotion surged through him and guilt bit down hard. Was this why he'd been able to make love to her—because there was no threat of commitment?

He disentangled himself from her warm embrace and sat back, dragging his hands over his hair, anger beginning to simmer in him. Anger at himself.

She reached up and touched his face with her fingertips, her eyes soft. She smiled. "Luke," she whispered. "It's okay, I wanted this."

He returned her smile, feeling suddenly overwhelmed. He fingered the small gold pendant nestling at her throat, noticing for the first time it was actually a collection of Chinese characters.

He lifted it on his fingers to take a closer look. "What does it mean, Jess?"

"It's the Chinese symbol for pride," she said. "My mother gave it to me when I was little. She wanted me to remember to always be proud of myself, of my culture, my heritage. She told me that no matter what, I must never allow other people to think they are somehow better than me because they have fathers." She laughed softly, a poignancy creeping into her eyes. "I think my mother was more embarrassed at not having a proper husband than I was at not having a father around."

"What happened to him?"

She gave a small shrug, causing her hair to cascade over her shoulder and swing in a dark curtain over her breast. "I don't really care what happened to him. He dumped my mother when he found out she was pregnant. He gave her cash and told her to go get an abortion."

"Who is your father, Jess?"

Her eyes flicked away. "I really don't think it matters."

"Hey—" he caught her chin, turned her face to him "—I'd like to know."

She hesitated.

"You made me share, Jess. We're equals here, right?" he said with mock solemnity.

She laughed. "Touché, Stone. It's not that I have anything to hide, I just don't like talking about him. He's now an entrepreneur in Hong Kong. My mother was his housekeeper and he turned her into his mistress." In spite of Jessica's laugh, she seemed unable to ward off the faint bitterness that laced into her voice with her next words. "But when she got pregnant with me, he gave her cash, put her on a plane, and sent her to a doctor he knew personally in the U.K. to get an abortion. He apparently said it would kill his reputation and wreck his marriage if people found out my mom was pregnant with his child."

"What did your mother do?"

Jess snorted gently. "She got on the plane, kept the cash and kept me. She went to live near London with distant family relations in the Chinese community."

"What does your father do, exactly?" Luke heard the rough edge permeating his voice, felt his protective instincts surface, and he knew it was a bad sign. It showed he'd somehow become invested in this woman. He wanted to fix things for her that went well beyond his realm.

She blew air out slowly. "He was in politics. Now he's into real estate, big casinos."

"What's his name?"

"His name doesn't matter, Luke. I really don't want it to matter. He threatened my mother with ruin when he found out she'd given birth to a daughter. He said if she ever came near him or made any claim on him whatsoever, he would deny everything and destroy her." She lifted her exotic amber eyes to his. "So there you have it. He really doesn't exist to me."

But Luke could see in her eyes that he did.

"Why did she tell you about him?"

"I asked. I wanted to know who my father was. Not that I

wanted anything from him. I just needed to know where I came from."

"And your mother never contacted him for support?"

Jessica shook her head. "She was too proud. She did it all on her own, working three jobs to get me through school and into university. She struggled and I wanted to show her that her efforts were worth gold to me. I wanted to make her proud. I *needed* to do well, Luke. I worked my butt off to get my job with the BBC and I was climbing all the way to the top." Fire flashed in her eyes as she spoke. "That's why it killed me when the damn Triad took everything from me, including my job and my reputation."

"But they didn't take your pride, Jess," he whispered, his eyes growing hot with affection for her.

She glanced away, then sat up suddenly and pulled the blanket over her shoulders. Her eyes flared to his, something suddenly very raw in them. "I can't handle the fact that I will never see her again." Moisture started to glimmer in her eyes. "I can't get on that chopper."

Luke tried to swallow the ball of emotion swelling in his throat. "You must, Jess," he whispered, feeling sick. "I can't protect you from them forever."

Like he hadn't been able to protect Rebecca and his son.

She turned away sharply, stared at the dying coals. He could see she was struggling to hold it all in.

"Why were you in Shanghai, Jess?" he asked quietly. "Why did you go there in the first place?"

Her eyes whipped back to his, surprise rippling through her features. "I…I wanted to become fluent in Chinese. I wanted to get in touch with that aspect of my heritage—"

"You're part British, too, you know? I think you wanted to get a job near your father, somewhere close where he'd be forced to notice you." He watched her eyes closely as he spoke. "Perhaps you even wanted your face to mock him from the television in his house, right under his nose, covering issues that pertained to him. You wanted him to see you were doing just fine—great, in fact—in spite of him."

She flushed slightly and Luke knew he was right.

"So maybe that was part of it. What? You're the shrink now?"

"What's his name, Jess?" he asked again.

"Archer Stonaway," she said finally, avoiding his eyes. "He used to be the British consul-general in Hong Kong. He was always into real estate and when he stepped away from the diplomatic post, he remained in Hong Kong and continued to build his business empire."

A cold sinking feeling leached through Luke. "Look at me, Jess."

She lifted her eyes.

"Was he in office when you were abducted?"

"Yes. Why?"

Luke's brain began to race.

"What are you thinking, Luke? That there's some connection? Because there isn't. I don't think Archer Stonaway even knows who I am in spite of my work in China. And it was the British Embassy in Shanghai that dealt with my case, not Hong Kong."

He reached for his pants and stood up. "You're right, it's probably nothing." He checked his watch. "You need to get dressed, we must leave by daybreak. And, Jess, no more logs on the fire. I don't want smoke."

He pulled on his coat and stepped into the biting cold dawn, his breath crystallizing in the air. It had stopped snowing and the sky had cleared, stars sprinkling a violet dome that heralded the coming dawn.

Luke swore softly and rammed his hands deep into his pockets as he trudged through thick snow, breaking trail toward the shed where he'd seen the snowmobile.

He'd crossed the line big-time.

Hell alone knew what was going to come next, because this was uncharted territory for him. All he could do now was try to keep a clear head and focus on the immediate task—delivering Jessica. And he had only two hours to do it.

If he failed to get her on that chopper, he'd be failing her. Just as he'd failed Rebecca.

There was no way it could be otherwise, thought Luke as he ripped back the cover that protected the sled. He was a clear Dragon Heads target now; no one would ever be safe around him—*especially* if he cared for them.

Jessica rummaged through the supply cupboard and found some packets of instant oatmeal and coffee. No tea.

She stilled, packets in hand, wondering about the whiskey bottle last night, about the way Luke had reacted.

Jessica now suspected his ripped body and obsession with health had more to do with staying in emotional control than physical shape. She wondered just how hard it must have been for him after his wife died.

Clearly he was still struggling with guilt. Still afraid of slipping somehow. Afraid, even, of his own passion. She tore open the packet, emptied the oats into an enamel bowl, and tears welled suddenly in her eyes.

Damn. She smudged them away quickly.

But the emotion had taken hold of her. She squeezed her eyes shut, and leaned her hands on the small kitchen counter, trying to control herself. She didn't want to leave him.

She wanted more.

She suspected he did, too.

He needed someone to lean on just as much as she did.

Jessica blew air out slowly.

She didn't have a choice. Or did she?

Maybe she *would* rather risk her life. Surely that was her choice, and not his.

Luke found a supply of diesel fuel and filled the snowmobile tank, his mind ticking fast.

An RCMP chopper would be in the air as soon as there was enough light. There was no way he and Jessica could use the SUV, not with the amount of snow that had fallen in the night. Besides, there was only one road in and out of this valley. They'd be sitting ducks from the air.

The snow would have blanketed any trace of their movements last night, and his SUV was well buried. However, RCMP spotters would soon see footprints around the cabin from the air and send someone to investigate. He and Jessica needed to move soon, before dawn. A snowmobile was the best way to do it—the only way at their disposal right now.

Luke sealed the fuel tank and turned the ignition. The two-stroke engine coughed and sputtered blue smoke for a tense moment, before rolling over and settling into a low, throaty growl.

Good. Luke glanced up at the shed shelves, saw helmets. They would provide additional disguise, as would the old hunting clothes Jessica was wearing. He'd get her to braid her hair and tuck it under her jacket.

A shiver chased over his skin as the chill winter morning penetrated his clothes. Clear skies had brought an even sharper drop in temperature. It was maybe three degrees, well below freezing. This was good, though. The rivers would be solid. It would facilitate a fast route to the airfield, one that stayed well clear of the road.

"Luke?"

He stilled, then forced himself to glance round into her whiskey eyes, worried his resolve would weaken when he did.

Her cheeks were pink from cold. She looked so beautiful.

"I saw a deer," she said with a ripple of innocent pleasure in her voice that caught him right in the gut. "It peered right in the window while I was making breakfast. God," she said, turning and taking in the pristine sparkling wilderness of a hushed predawn winter wonderland. "It's like a whole new world—utterly glorious."

It was a beautiful world right now, thought Luke, mostly because she was standing in it. He cleared his throat. "Sun will bust over those mountains any minute. We should leave."

Her smiled faded. So did the gold light in her eyes. She nodded slightly. "Want some breakfast before we go?"

"No time." He handed her a helmet. "Here, take this. Go

get what you need inside. Braid your hair and tuck it under your jacket."

She waited a beat, watching him with unwavering, luminous eyes. Then she turned abruptly and left, tramping back through the thigh-deep drifts to the cabin.

Luke gritted his teeth. Cool, detached and calm—that's what he needed to be if he wanted to get her out of here alive.

But he was going to miss her. More than he should after knowing her such a short while. Some people had that kind of impact on one's life.

But *he* didn't want her to miss *him*.

Jessica was going to have enough sadness. She was going to lose her identity, everything that was familiar and defined her. The last thing he wanted to do was compound her problems.

It would be best if she believed that she was just another job to him, just another woman he'd slept with.

It would be best for him, too.

With a bitter taste in his mouth, Luke placed a call to Jacques Sauvage.

"Listen up, mate, we have a problem," he said tonelessly. "We've been compromised. Our triad friends got wind of where we were staying, came straight for the hotel, and directly to our room. Happened as soon as the road reopened in the early a.m., which means there's no way we were followed. They knew *exactly* where to find us, Sauvage."

"What happened?"

"Left a few bodies on our way out, I'm afraid. I'm going to have some serious enemies when I'm done here, Sauvage, and I am not happy about it."

"What is your location now?"

He didn't want to say. "I'm thinking it's our phone system that might be bugged. I don't know how else those guys knew where to find us last night."

"Our sat system uses the most advanced military encryption technology available. We check continuously for breaches—"

"Check again, Sauvage, because *something* is going on."

Jacques was silent for a moment. "*Ça va*, I'll get our techs to take another look. In the meantime you're on schedule for the pickup?"

"No worries, mate. It's as good as in the bag. Otherwise I'm going radio silent. Contact me when you have confirmation our communication is secure."

Luke signed off and paused a moment, holding the phone. If the Triad knew where to find them last night, they could also know about the pickup.

But until he could figure out how they were being compromised, there was no point in trying to change the rendezvous. The best he could hope for was that the CIA brought enough firepower to ward off a possible attack.

Meanwhile, he and Jessica would use surprise. They would work their way along the valley via the dyking system and agricultural fields and cross the river at a point well beyond the airport, then backtrack in an approach from the rear. From there they'd advance cautiously through the woods, which would offer cover and provide a clean sight line to the airstrip and helipad. If anything looked like it was going to go sideways, they could slip back into dense forest and traverse mountainous terrain no SUV could access. The dense forest would also provide cover if they were pursued by air.

Luke made his way back to the cabin, where he avoided Jessica's eyes as he packed his gear. He took some water bottles and a couple of flares from the supply cupboard and he checked and loaded his weapon before shouldering his pack. "Time to go," he said.

Her eyes probed his, searching for the man she'd connected with only an hour earlier. Luke clenched his jaw and turned his back on her before she could glimpse how he really felt.

As they raced over a pristine landscape transformed by storm snow, the sun crested over the mountaintops in a crashing symphony of gold, rippling down into the valley, painting the snow in tones of champagne and honey, backlighting a high ridge of frozen white conifers and making them shimmer as if with crystal fire.

Luke released the throttle, feeling the spinning cleats bite into snow as they were propelled at high speed along the dykes that lined the wide frozen river. Jessica had her arms tight around his waist, her legs straddling him.

The crisp air was pine-scented and intoxicating.

Luke opened the throttle further, wanting to cross private land as fast as he could before an early-rising farmer saw them and alerted authorities. Going flat out on the snowmobile, Luke could feel the g-force loading heavily in his centre. It was a solid and familiar sensation of power. Combined with the angry throbbing of the two-stroke engine between his legs and control of the throttle in his fist, a wild kind of angry energy soared up inside him.

And the closer they got to the airport, the more he wanted to veer sharply and irresponsibly off course, hammerhead straight up into the vaulted mountain peaks where he could find a place to hide Jessica.

But it was madness. He knew these mountains, and he knew what was in the forecast. They'd never last without supplies.

He also knew that gunning into the mountains would be just another way for him to run from his own ghosts. He had to face this. He had to hand her over, let her go.

He came to a stop up high on a ridge overlooking the valley, from where he was able to see the airport in the distance. He took his scopes from his pack and handed Jessica a bottle of water.

She removed her helmet, her black braid shining in the bright morning sunlight as though sprinkled with a million microscopic blue diamonds. Her cheeks were flushed and her skin translucent, her gold eyes bright with the exhilaration of the ride.

Luke stilled, captivated by the sight of her.

For a fleeting moment he realized *this* was the woman he could take on his solitary backcountry trips. This was the woman who could share an appreciation for his passions, his thrill for speed and wild things.

The thought shocked him.

He'd never dreamed he'd actually want anyone to breach his isolation. For the first time in the four years since the loss of his wife, Luke had encountered a woman who made him think of the future. But she was a woman he couldn't have.

A pain began to pound in his temple.

He needed to get rid of her soon. This was killing him.

Jessica threw back her head, downing half the bottle of water in one go. Luke could not resist watching her throat work as she swallowed heartily, and he felt his body stir in response. She wiped her mouth with the back of her glove and was about to pass the bottle to him, when she froze at what she saw in his eyes.

Luke quickly broke his gaze and raised his binoculars to his eyes. He scanned the distant valley below, forcing himself to focus. He could see no one at the airfield yet. But then he heard it—a remote *thuck thuck thuck* reverberating against the peaks—and his chest tightened.

"Is that the helicopter?" she whispered, shading her eyes and squinting up into sky.

He trained his binoculars on the chopper as it materialized out of the shimmering sunlight—sleek and black and unmarked. It banked and came in for a landing. "Yeah," he said. "That's her."

"And that's the airstrip down there?"

Luke nodded as he noted the dark clouds already forming behind the peaks of Mount Currie to the south. The next storm was riding in fast. He turned his scopes back to the valley, carefully scanning the dense forest fringe that lined the length of the snow-covered airstrip.

Nothing jumped out at him as unusual. He focused on the area around the helipad and hangars, then panned the strip of isolated road approaching the airport. He saw nothing of concern there, either. At least not from this vantage point.

"Luke," her voice broke into his concentration. "What if I *don't* get on the chopper?"

He lowered the glasses slowly. "You have to, Jess. Your life depends on it."

"I told you, I don't have a life if I go into CIA protection. Not the life I want."

He didn't know what to say. So he said nothing.

She glanced at the ground. He could see the uncertainty, the anxiety mounting in her, and it made him feel awkward.

"Do…you think that maybe if things were different, you and I…" She flushed slightly. "I mean, do you think there might have been a chance for us, in another place, another time?"

His mouth turned dry. "No, Jess, I don't," he lied coolly. "If you weren't going to disappear, this would never have happened."

Hurt—raw hurt—flashed hot and fast through her eyes.

Luke's heart torqued. "Jess…I told you, guys like me have no right to get involved. People close to me get hurt. I…we…shouldn't have…"

She shrugged dismissively. "Hey, it's okay. I needed to be held and you held me." She hesitated and then smiled sadly. "It was good, Luke. It felt so right, I thought that maybe…"

All he wanted to do was take her in his arms, hold her again. Forever. He cleared his throat. "I'm sorry."

She nodded, returned her eyes to the ground. "Me, too," she said softly.

They skirted through the trees encroaching along the northern boundary of the airstrip, coming closer to the gleaming black machine, its blades still rotating in slow sweeping circles as it waited for her.

Luke stopped the snowmobile and absorbed the scene ahead. Five men with rifles surrounded the craft. The pilot was inside.

Jessica's mouth went dry.

She glanced at Luke.

His hands were rock steady as he held the scopes. He was the most solid thing she'd come across in years. She sucked back a sudden wave of hurt. He'd made it clear—she was just a job, a ship in the night.

She'd been fool to say what she had. She was mortified the

words had even come out of her mouth. Not once had Luke led her on. Not once had he promised her anything different.

His mission was to save and deliver and as her bodyguard he was doing just that. Nothing more. Nothing less.

Making love had been her fault and she accepted full responsibility for that.

Even if she'd met him in a safe and innocuous situation she'd have been physically attracted to him. Luke Stone simply put other men in shadow.

But what really grabbed her by the throat was Luke's capacity for devotion.

That notion of forever, of something substantial and enduring, was like a holy grail for Jessica at the moment.

But right now she was facing an end. Not a forever.

She had to accept that.

He lowered his scopes. "Looks clean," he said. "You ready?"

Jessica inhaled sharply and nodded. "As ready as I'll ever be."

Chapter 10

Luke eased the throttle and ventured onto the frozen expanse, moving toward the waiting chopper at a steady, watchful pace, feeling Jessica's arms tighten around his waist.

Three of the men quickly repositioned to face them, surprised by the direction of their approach. The other two remained facing guard in the opposite direction.

As Luke neared, tension mounted and the rotor blades began to swing faster as the pilot readied for a rapid takeoff. Snow swirled in the increasing downdraft.

Suddenly, a black SUV materialized from behind a snowy rise in the distance. It swerved onto the open field and barreled toward the chopper, a wake of white powder boiling out behind it. Almost simultaneously, another vehicle bulleted out from the cover of a hangar. Both SUVs converged on the helipad in a rapid V formation as a third appeared on the airport approach road.

It took a second for the CIA officers to notice the movement. They swung round, weapons raised, and fired as the vehicles bore down on them. The men in the vehicles returned automatic gunfire as the rotor blades hit full speed and a blizzard of churning snow obscured vision.

Using the snow cloud for cover, Luke veered sideways, goosed his machine, gunning for the protection of a metal hangar.

A CIA officer went down as bullets rattled across the surface of the Kevlar-protected helicopter. A second agent fell in the hail of gunfire. The SUVs—clearly bulletproof themselves—continued advancing at a rapid clip.

Luke reached cover just as bullets sparked off the corner of the metal siding of the hangar.

He skidded to a stop, breathing hard, Jessica hanging on for dear life as the pilot began to lift off with the remaining CIA officers on board.

The chopper rose and banked, speeding at low altitude toward the forest. Luke wasn't sure if the attackers had seen him and Jessica through the swirling downdraft or if they thought Jessica was already on board. He held back behind the shed for a tense moment, calculating his enemy's next move.

That's when he heard the explosion. He spun round in shock as the helicopter whooshed into a violent ball of flame and tumbled from the sky, breaking into burning black pieces as it went down into the conifers. Acrid black smoke mushroomed into the air.

Luke immediately lowered his head and gunned his engine, shooting out from behind the hangar and making a beeline for the snowbank that led up to the road, smoke and flame providing diversion.

But as sled cleats propelled them up the bank, the first shot pinged into his machine. He swerved up onto the road and saw the third SUV making directly for them.

He veered immediately right, bulleting down the opposite bank toward the river, praying the ice would hold them when they hit. Sled skids hammered onto the frozen surface and lost grip as Luke tried to turn, sending them sliding laterally for several yards before the machine found purchase again.

It cost them precious seconds.

The black SUV appeared up on the ridge, a man got out and shouldered his weapon—a rocket propelled grenade launcher. Luke's heart shot to his throat.

It's what they must have used to bring the CIA chopper down.

He opened the throttle and raced full blast into a sharp curve in the river, knowing that when he hit the bend and turned hard left, his skids wouldn't grip, and they'd keep sliding, remaining in the man's crosshairs.

They hit the bend in the river just as the first grenade whizzed toward them. The snowmobile cleats suddenly bit into an unexpected patch of hard snow that had accumulated on the surface of the ice. It gave Luke the purchase he needed and he lurched full speed into the corner, shooting up the opposite riverbank as the grenade exploded into the ice behind them.

He kept going, hurtling across farmland, aiming for a ridge of trees and cluster of outbuildings, at the same time moving diametrically away from the road, making it impossible for the vehicles to follow them immediately.

He could see all three SUVs now racing in a row along the road on the ridge in the distance. He and Jessica were trapped in the valley.

As he reached the cover of the trees, Luke slowed to a steady chug and cautiously approached the farm outbuildings. A rusting red flatbed truck was parked in an open barn near a cattle pen. Several cows with thick winter coats grazed from a trough, warm mud at their feet churned and black against the snow. Across the snowy field, a thin wisp of smoke curled up from the chimney of a house in the distance. Luke could see no other sign of human activity.

He drew to a stop just outside the barn, out of sight from the house.

Their shortcut over farmland had bought them time, but the triad vehicles would be coming this way via road any moment.

"You okay?" he asked Jessica.

Her skin was bloodless and her eyes wide behind her visor, but she nodded.

A bitter rage sliced through Luke as he pulled off his helmet, thinking how close he'd come to getting her killed. It fed something else in him—a fierce determination to protect her at whatever cost—and with it came a hot thrill. *He still had her.*

He still had a chance.

He'd been granted a reprieve and this time he wasn't going to blow it.

Luke was going to keep this woman safe or he would die trying. And he was going renegade. No FDS. No CIA.

Not until he had a handle on who was pulling the strings.

They now had only two options. They could head north into the backcountry, perhaps make it over the mountains and out near the Fraser River. Luke peered up at the massive peaks of Mount Currie that loomed over the valley.

The sky behind the mountain was already turning black and a chill wind strengthening, redolent of the approaching storm front. They had no supplies. They'd be socked in over the mountains and freeze to death.

The only other option was to step out into the open and hide in plain sight. Luke was good at this. In his experience, people tended to see what they expected to see. But you needed a certain boldness to pull it off. Any slip in confidence would alert the enemy. He hoped Jessica was up to it.

First step was transport.

He glanced at the old flatbed piled with hay bales. There wasn't much crime in this valley known worldwide for its seed potatoes—he'd bet the key was still in the ignition. The barn was also close to the road, which had been plowed. A smile tugged at his lips.

He flicked his eyes to Jess. "Wanna go rural?" he whispered.

Her eyes widened. "You mean take *that thing?*"

He nodded.

Jessica saw a flicker of amusement in his eyes and it suddenly bolstered her. Luke Stone was so totally in control she'd swear he enjoyed this.

If Luke had been just a few seconds slower, a little less sharp in thinking, a little less proficient on the sled—they'd both have gone up in a ball of fire like the CIA operatives and pilot.

Jessica was devastated by what had happened to those men, but at the same time, she was physically exhilarated at having cheated death, at just being alive. Breathing this cold mountain air. And still being with him.

It was a damn sight better than the alternatives.

"Stash our helmets behind those bales over there," he whispered, handing her his helmet. "And get rid of the jacket—they've seen it."

They entered the barn and Luke checked the door of the truck as she hid their gear. "It's open," he whispered. "Key's inside."

But they both tensed as the front door of the house in the distance opened and snatches of a woman's voice reached them. A German shepherd barreled out the door and over the snowy field, barking furiously, making straight for the old barn.

"The dog knows we're here," she whispered.

Luke placed his hand on her arm. "Stay calm. Get in the truck."

The dog rounded the corner and froze in an aggressive stance, growling and baring teeth. Luke reached for his weapon, and Jessica's heart pounded as she backed slowly toward the truck.

"It's okay boy," Luke whispered, slowly extending his left hand even as his right remained at his gun belt. "We're not going to hurt you."

Jessica watched as the dog hesitated, then cocked his ears in question. He was still growling, but his body began to do a cautious body wiggle as he advanced slowly to sniff Luke's hand.

"You're just scared, aren't you, pooch?" Luke said as he began to scratch behind the dog's ear. The animal's tail started to twist in big loopy circles as his body wiggle intensified. Jessica realized then that the dog was probably quite young, simply afraid.

Like she was.

"Winston, eh?" said Luke, reading the dog's name on the tag at his collar. "Want to come for a ride, Winston?"

"You have *got* to be kidding!" she hissed from the truck.

He flicked his eyes to her. "It's the last thing they'll expect. He'll seal our cover."

Luke moved round to the driver's side of the flatbed, and opened the door with a rusty creak. Winston leaped into the truck in front of him and snuggled up against Jessica, his tail thumping expectantly on the seat, pink tongue lolling happily. She could swear the dog was smiling.

Luke tossed his pack into the truck cab and climbed in after it, grinning as he reached for the key in the ignition. "Get the sunglasses and wool hat from my pack, and pull the hat low over your head, tuck your hair under that plaid shirt," he said as he turned the key.

Jessica had ditched Luke's down jacket and was already shivering in the flannel hunting shirt they'd borrowed from the cabin.

"We'll pick up some warmer stuff later," he said as the truck engine cranked over and spluttered to a rough rumble. Luke shifted it into gear and eased the vehicle out into the snow. The sunlight was wickedly harsh, glaring off acres of crystalline snow and ice, and Jessica was glad for the dark shades.

"Pass me that old hat and the glasses lying in the back there," Luke said as he edged the flatbed up onto the road and they began to drive toward the village at a frustratingly slow crawl.

Jessica handed Luke the sunglasses and cowboy hat, which he rammed low over his head. He threw her a wicked look and a smile that made his eyes twinkle with unspeakable mischief.

Her heart did a little tumble in her chest. "How long do you think it'll be before they see their truck is missing?"

Luke shrugged. "Could be a while. The house was far back enough and with the windows closed they may not have heard the engine. Plus the barn entrance faced away from the house. We should be good for a few minutes."

"Right. A few minutes." Tension began to wind tight inside Jessica as they trundled along the road, bits of hay flying off behind them in the wind. "Can't you go any faster?"

"Think about it, Jess—a flatbed speeding somewhere at the

same time as our escape? Going fast will just trigger a chase response. The key is to stay calm." He glanced into the rearview mirror. "Here they come now."

Her throat turned dry and her heart began to slam. She spun round and peered out the back of the cab. Three sleek SUVs materialized on the horizon. They were coming fast along the straight ribbon of road.

"Don't look, Jess."

She could barely breathe. "They'll see us."

He nodded. "That's the idea." He turned on the radio found a music channel, and slowed to an even more infuriating pace. Jessica thought she might implode with the strain. Beads of perspiration formed along her brow under her hat, in spite of the cold; her palms turned clammy.

"Luke, please, you're killing me. Go just a *little* bit faster."

His features turned serious. "Jessica, trust me, your life depends on you staying calm right now. People see what they expect to see, and the devil is in the little details—the dog, the music, the hay bales. The unhurried speed. Think of them as a magician's sleight of hand. When you see those things, you miss the rest."

She swallowed.

"Just look straight ahead. Smile. Relax."

Yeah, right. Adrenaline from the snowmobile chase was still screaming through her blood. Every instinct in her body was howling to flee. And fast. "Are they getting near?" She had to force herself not to turn around and see for herself.

"Almost on us. Easy now."

"Luke," she hissed in a panic. "Where can we go in this thing, anyway? Those people are going to see it's missing. The cops will be alerted. I mean, we're in a big rusty flatbed with hay bales and a dog! We're as obvious as a pink bloody elephant."

"That's the point of hiding in plain sight, Jess. Don't worry, we'll ditch the flatbed, pick up a rental." He glanced into the rearview mirror again. "Here they come. Relax."

Jessica felt as though she was going to throw up from nerves.

She'd had her fill over the last few days and she wasn't sure just how much more of this madness she was built to take.

She heard the SUVs slowing behind their truck. She felt dizzy. Her knuckles were white where she gripped the door handle. Winston was dribbling on her.

Luke lowered the shades over his eyes, turned up a Western song on the radio and began to hum along as he wound down his window and casually waved them on. He steered the flatbed to the side of the road as he did, making room for them to pass.

Oh, God, he was attracting attention to them now! How did he handle this? It was enough to make her puke. Luke Stone must *live* for this kind of thrill. She wondered how a woman could possibly coexist with a guy like that.

The first SUV in the convoy drew level with them, keeping pace, the occupants invisible behind dark windows. Jessica held her breath. "Don't look at them, Jess," Luke growled through his smile. "Keep looking straight ahead." He raised his hand in greeting, and smiled at the men. Suddenly the convoy sped up and passed.

Jessica's stomach swooped. She slumped back in the seat, and tears filled her eyes.

She closed them for a moment, struggling to find her breath again. "I…I guess they don't recognize your face."

"Guess they saw what they expected—a farmer and a dog and his wife in their truck."

His wife.

Jessica was reminded again of Luke's capacity for love and loyalty. With her emotional defenses already shot to high heaven, the thought overwhelmed her. "You're something else, you know that?" she said.

He slid his eyes over to her, and grinned. "You're no slouch yourself, Jessica Chan." He reached for her knee and gave it a squeeze. "You did good." His smile broadened. "Again."

He put both hands on the old wheel and Jessica felt they had just bonded in yet a deeper way. It was going to be even more difficult to extract herself from this strange partnership now.

As they neared the small farming village, two fire engines, an ambulance, and a police cruiser with sirens screaming blasted past them in the opposite direction.

They were heading for the carnage at the deserted airport, as once again she and Luke escaped the scene.

"What are we going to do with Winston?" she asked as they entered the outskirts of Pemberton village.

"You want a dog?"

"Not someone else's!"

He crooked a brow. "But you *would* like a dog?"

She rubbed her hand over her eyes, trying to relieve tension. "I've always wanted a dog," she said. "All my life. Guess it wasn't in my cards."

"I'd like a dog," he said.

Her eyes shot to him. "I thought you had issues putting down roots? I thought you said people like you can't commit."

"That's why I *don't* have a dog." He turned off the road into a parking lot for a time-share lodge. "Doesn't mean I wouldn't like one."

Jessica studied his profile. He'd just told her a lot about himself in that statement.

Twenty minutes later, Luke and Jessica were in a rental sedan heading south on Highway 99, back toward the ski resort of Whistler, skis and snowboard strapped to the roof.

The time-share lodge where they'd rented the car offered special ski package combos—which meant their vehicles came with the option of ski rentals. As Luke had pointed out, no one expected a couple on the run to rent ski gear. Jessica was getting the hang of this now—the devil was in the details.

They'd left Winston at the lodge with the truck parked right out front. There was a phone number on his tag and when lodge staff finally got around to noticing the barking dog had been abandoned, they would call his owners who would get their truck and their pet back in one package.

The plan was to leave this rental in Whistler and pick up another under a false name before heading on to Vancouver. It would be at least two days before the lodge expected the return of their rental and by then Luke and Jessica would be long gone.

Jessica was incredibly nervous about returning to the city, but Luke had insisted hiding there in plain sight was a far better option than dying in the wilderness or becoming obvious in a smaller community while he tried to figure out their next steps.

The next storm front was already socking them in, wipers barely keeping up with the accumulation of snow. A chopper *thucked* steadily in the low cloud somewhere above them, but they were hidden from visibility.

"What about police road blocks?" she asked.

"We'll take them as they come," he said. "But the cops are going to be pretty tied up trying to figure what went down with the helicopter. It'll be some hours before they manage to get a forensics team from Vancouver up there in this weather."

Jessica finally allowed herself to relax into the warmth of the car. There was no more doubt—she trusted him implicitly. Exhausted, she fell into a deep sleep.

Luke nudged Jessica awake in Squamish. They'd switched vehicles about 30 miles back and she'd gone right back to sleep. "Wait in the car while I pick up some gear," he said.

She opened her eyes sleepily. "What kind of gear?"

"Stuff to disguise ourselves. Can't walk into the hotel wearing that." He motioned to her oversize loggers shirt and pants, and she couldn't help smiling at him. "I feel like Bonnie and Clyde," she said, rubbing her eyes.

"Didn't end too well for them, did it?"

"Guess not," she said. Those road movies never did end well. Maybe there was a reason for that. Maybe there was only so far you *could* run.

Still, she'd rather be on the lam with Luke Stone than sitting in a CIA holding room. At least she felt *alive,* more so than she had in years.

Jessica was beginning to think going down in a hailstorm of bullets with Luke Stone at her side was far preferable to a fake existence in a witness protection program.

He grabbed her face in both hands suddenly and kissed her hard on the mouth. He pulled back, his eyes strangely light. "God, Jess, I'm glad I didn't hand you over back there."

And then he was gone.

Jessica's heart thudded. As she watched him stride into the big discount store, she couldn't resist a smile. It was the last place on earth she'd expect to see a man like Luke Stone.

She hadn't expected to see that kind of emotion in his eyes, either.

Beyond her better judgment, she'd fallen for her protector.

Chapter 11

Luke's phone rang as he exited the store with his loot—a couple of big jackets to keep them warm until they reached Vancouver, a scarf for Jessica, a pair of scissors, some bleach, hair dye, makeup, glasses and a few other accessories. He'd collect everything else he needed in the city.

He checked the phone ID. It was Jacques. Luke had told his boss to maintain radio silence until he was one-hundred percent certain the line was secure. Jacques must have deemed the line safe.

"Yeah?" Luke said cautiously, moving to a secluded corner outside the store as he answered.

"Stone, our techs went through the sat system inside and out—the encryption is secure, absolutely no electronic evidence of eavesdropping."

"You sure?"

"As sure as we can be. We need to talk. I just heard from Weston. He lost five men and a pilot and we've got the Canadian feds crawling all over this. CSIS, too. What in hell happened?"

Luke hesitated. CSIS was the Canadian equivalent to the CIA—this just kept getting bigger.

And if their phone system wasn't bugged, then how had the information been getting out?

He glanced at their rental car in the snow-covered parking lot. There was just no way he was going to put her at risk like that again.

He'd made the fatal mistake of beginning to care. She was no longer his principal. She was a woman he was simply compelled to look after and it was too damn late to change that fact now.

"Triad got to the chopper before we did," he said quietly.

Jacques swore. "The principal?"

"Intact. Look, Sauvage, if you're convinced our communication is secure, then the leak has *got* to be coming from the CIA end. I don't see any other explanation."

"Like I said, Weston closed the circle on this after Rehnquist's assassination in Shanghai. It's just him and a few key personnel in the loop. I am liaising with him directly. He's asked for personal updates every step of the way as part of this contract."

"Well, his loop is not tight enough," said Luke. "And I can't hand Jessica Chan over to the CIA until we know who in that loop of Weston's is a mole. We're going to ground, Sauvage."

Jacques was quiet for a moment. "Stone, don't go renegade on me now. You do need to bring her in."

"Not until we know who the mole is."

Jacques exhaled. "All right. We bring her to São Diogo then, to the FDS base. We hold her on the island and halt communication with the agency until Weston sorts out any security breach his end. Then we deliver her stateside. Where are you? Can you get to an airport?"

Luke didn't answer. He stared at the car, something hardening in his chest. "Any word on The Chemist's ID?" he asked. "Anything in those passenger manifests?"

"Not yet."

"Have you told Weston we have the photographs that identified Ben Woo?"

"Negative."

"Let's keep it that way."

"We plan to."

Luke forced out air, pulling his concentration into focus. "Can you do me a favor, Sauvage? Can you see what your techs can dig up on Archer Stonaway, ex-British consul-general for Hong Kong. He's Jessica Chan's father."

"Anything particular you're looking for?"

"Just anything that throws up flags. He's into Hong Kong real estate—casinos in particular."

"Hong Kong casinos are Xiang's turf."

"Exactly. If there's a link between Stonaway and Xiang, we need to know about it. I'll check in when I can." Luke signed off. This time he wasn't telling a damn soul where they were going—not until he knew exactly who the good guys were. And the bad guys.

It wasn't that Luke didn't trust Jacques, but his boss was compelled to keep CIA director Blake Weston personally informed on every little detail of this contract and Luke was getting a bad feeling about Weston himself.

Jessica was relieved to see her bodyguard finally striding back over the parking lot, armed with shopping bags.

He handed her the packages as he climbed in, slamming his door shut behind him. She opened one, pulled out a thickly padded jacket and grinned. "Thank you, I'm freezing." Then she chuckled as she saw the label. "It's made in China."

"So is most of the stuff in that store," he said, starting the ignition.

"You know it's the Chinese New Year?"

"I hadn't really thought about it," he said, steering back onto the snowy highway.

Jessica studied the little red dragon on the label, suddenly feeling nostalgic. "My mother always used to prepare a feast for us," she said softly. "Traditionally the celebrations go on for several days, but the big day is when they hold the parade in

Chinatown. It's a time families get together." She glanced up as emotion surged through her chest. "It's been over a week since I spoke to her, Luke. She's going to wonder why I haven't called."

"It wouldn't be wise, Jess."

"How does the CIA intend to explain my disappearance to her?"

Luke shot her a look. "You know how these things work."

Anger bubbled inside her. "Right. They'll bring her some false evidence of my death."

He reached out and squeezed her hand.

Jessica slumped back in her seat, packages still on her lap, so frustrated she wanted to scream.

"They got a match," he said quietly, as he rounded yet another hairpin bend that hugged the ragged cliffs.

"What?"

"The FDS crew has positively identified Xiang-Li and the man obscured by shadow in your photos. He's Ben Woo, personal assistant to the Chinese deputy consul-general in San Francisco."

Jessica's mouth dropped open as she swiveled in her seat. "How long were you going to wait before telling me this?"

"I'm telling you now."

"That's the proof I've been looking for, Luke! That elements of the Chinese government are clearly connected to the Dragon Heads Triad. I can't believe you didn't tell me this right away." She wondered what *else* he was keeping from her, her trust in him beginning to waver slightly. "Why do you think Woo is here?"

"A government official meeting with a global triad leader and an alleged assassin for the Chinese government? My guess is that there's some kind of political assassination going down."

Her breath lodged sharply in her chest. "Is…the FDS going to pass this to the CIA?"

He shook his head. "Not until we figure out who has been compromising us, Jess."

Relief rushed through her, then stress swallowed it right back up again. She tried to steady her breath. "Who do you think they might assassinate?"

"I have no idea." He chewed on his cheek, thinking. "We already know the Dragon Heads are colonizing globally. They've taken over existing crime networks—both tongs and triads—in several major countries. Most recently the Circle K in Australia—"

"The triad that killed your wife?"

He nodded.

She studied his unyielding profile, his beautiful strong hands on the wheel. So in control. She *had* to keep trusting this man. They were locked into this together no matter which way you looked at it.

Before she even realized she was doing it, Jessica had reached out and placed her hand on his knee. His eyes flicked to hers and held a moment.

"Like I was saying," he said, switching back to the subject. "If the Dragon Heads are still aggressively expanding, they may be making a move on Pacific Northwest turf. And that means it might be a local triad or tong head they want to assassinate."

"But why bring in The Chemist? They could surely have found someone local."

"I don't know. But if a covert faction of the Chinese Communist Party *is* behind this Dragon Heads push into North America, and if the Dragon Heads *do* manage to take control of Asian organized crime in North America, it would give the Chinese government unprecedented access to the United States. And if the Chinese Communist Party starts using Dragon Heads networks to push a covert political agenda from within the U.S., we could have the start of a nice little cold war on our hands."

Jessica whistled softly. "This could be one of the biggest turf wars in history, with serious international political implications."

"Potentially." Luke paused for several beats. "Jacques wants me to get you out of here, Jess. He wants me take you to the FDS base on São Diogo Island, off the coast of Angola."

"And then what?"

"Once the CIA cleans up its security breach, we can hand you over to the Americans."

She sat quietly, staring at the road ahead. "I'm not going."

He shot a look at her.

"I am not going into witness protection, Luke. I've made up my mind."

He said nothing. Drove with hands tight on the wheel, fog swirling into the yellow beam of their headlights, snow turning to slush as they neared the lights of the city and the sky grew dark.

"You can't make me," she said suddenly, as if to convince herself. "It's my life. My choice."

He started to say something, hesitated, then spoke. "I should also tell you that I asked the FDS to check into your father's background."

She twisted sharply to face him. *"Why?"*

"Archer Stonaway is politically connected and he's into big casino real estate in Hong Kong. That's Xiang-Li's traditional turf, Jess. Xiang is Hong Kong's casino king. From mainland China, he effectively controls the entire industry. He even has half the Hong Kong police force under his control. There is very little in the casino industry that *isn't* touched by him."

"That doesn't mean my father is somehow involved in this."

"Why are you trying to protect him?"

"I…I'm not."

"Listen to yourself, Jess."

"I…I just don't want to believe he'd actually try to hurt me, Luke. Presuming he even knows who I am."

"I'm just covering the bases. We'd be remiss to not look for the links."

Jessica fingered the pendant at her neck. No matter how much she tried to pretend her father had no impact on her concept of identity, he did. Archer Stonaway had disowned her before she was even born and she hated what he'd done to her mother. Everything Jessica had ever strived for in life had been a way of defying her background, of proving she was worthy. Proud.

Something steeled in Jessica as she thought of her mother,

the meaning of the Chinese characters on her chain. The notion her father might be involved with Xiang-Li—in whatever capacity—simply fueled her anger and zeal to fight back, to claim what was hers.

It made her even more determined to never enter a protection program.

But Jessica also knew that Luke was as equally committed to his mission—keeping her alive.

She and Luke might be inextricably bound against one common enemy, but their approaches to that battle were diverging fast.

Luke drove into the heart of downtown Vancouver, the irony of their situation not lost on him. He was willing to die to get Jessica into protection, but she was prepared to give her life in order to stay free.

"We're staying *here?*" she said as he turned into the entrance of the city's most exclusive hotel. "Wouldn't it be better to stay in some fleabag motel on the outskirts of town?"

"It's exactly what they'd expect," he said, drawing to a stop under the golden lights of the hotel marquee. "There's lipstick in the shopping bag, Jess. Put it on. Scarf and sunglasses, too."

"Ugh," she said staring in horror at the shade of lipstick he'd bought. "This is awful. Ruby Passion? You actually want me to wear this?"

"I do," he said with a grin in spite of the conflict churning in his gut.

She snorted as she took the oversize sunglasses he'd bought out of the bag. "With these shades and scarf and that bright red lipstick, I'm going to look like some ludicrous Greta Garbo wannabe."

He chuckled. "Exactly. And a hotel like this will bend over backward to protect your anonymity if they suspect you're trying to duck somewhere incognito in a hurry. Trust me, Mrs. Smith."

She made a mock scowl. "You could pick a more original alias, you know?"

He unlocked the door. "It's one I have on file. For the duration of our stay, we're the Smiths. As soon as we're booked in, you go straight for the elevator and up to our room," Luke said as a uniformed valet stepped forward.

"What about you?" She said, pulling down the visor and quickly applying the bright red lipstick.

He ignored her question. "Do you know how to use a handgun, Jess?" he whispered urgently as the valet neared.

She stilled, holding the lipstick midair, her eyes suddenly dark. "I learned once. For a story I was working on."

"Good. Make sure your hair is covered, quick."

The valet reached for the door.

Luke slipped his arm around her waist as they approached the check-in desk. "The Ruby Passion looks fabulous," he murmured against her cheek.

Heat rippled through her stomach. "You actually *like* it?" she whispered.

"I'm afraid I'm not above being seduced by a bit of vamp, my dear," he said softly, before turning his attention to the check-in clerk and asking for a deluxe suite.

Once they'd signed in, Luke walked her over to the bank of bronzed elevators. "Take this up, will you?" he said shouldering off his pack. He leaned down as if to kiss her and Jessica braced in anticipation of the contact. But instead, he murmured sensually over her mouth. "My gun is in the pack. Keep it with you. Use it if you have to."

Jessica closed her eyes briefly and nodded, desire and fear tingling in her stomach. "Where are you going while I go to the room?"

"To get some couture for Mr. and Mrs. Smith."

"You do *not* expect me to call you Mr. Smith, do you?"

He laughed and left her standing alone at the elevators with his gun.

* * *

Jessica watched him step through the hotel's revolving glass doors and disappear into the night, a familiar sense of isolation blanketing her. Except this time the sense of abandonment was worse.

She wanted to end this madness. For good. She'd been lonely for far too long and being with Luke had made her hungry for something more in her life. Maybe even a future with him.

But she knew it couldn't be so. He'd pretty much told her flat out he'd never make a commitment.

In an effort to put the crazy notion out of her mind, she snagged a few copies of the local newspapers from the courtesy rack alongside the elevators as the bell pinged softy.

Stepping through the gleaming bronze doors, she studied the front page of the Chinese Independent Press as the car began to climb.

The main story was about the New Year parade at noon tomorrow. Jessica felt a small tug in her heart. Her mother would be starting to really worry now.

She scanned the editorial page as the elevator lights blipped steadily upward toward the 20th floor, recalling the time she'd met the editor. That interview had been her very first assignment with the small television station at which Stephanie had secured her a job.

Jessica had felt demeaned by the assignment. She'd long passed the stage of community reporting and she knew the piece had been dumped on her because she could speak Chinese and the editor barely spoke any English.

She'd ended up being pleasantly surprised, however. It turned out the editor had closely followed the news reports about her abduction in Shanghai and had been greatly honored to meet her. That day Jessica felt she'd gained an ally, her first sense of community in her new city. Strangely, it had given her the strength to stay the course in Vancouver.

And it had all been going okay until that fateful morning she'd seen Xiang-Li and The Chemist in Chinatown and her world had come to a clean stand-still. And then Stephanie had been killed.

She folded the newspaper, an acrid taste in her mouth, and stepped out into the hallway, fingering her key-card as she counted the numbers on the suite doors.

With the loaded gun just within reach, Jessica sank her body deep into the warm water and fragrant bath bubbles of an enormous Jacuzzi tub, desperate to leach out the cold that had penetrated to her bones.

The suite Luke had secured was glorious—complete with living and dining area, full bar, two rooms with king beds, fire crackling in a hearth and a commanding view over the city through floor-to-ceiling windows.

The bathroom was no less luxurious, done in gold and cream, mirrors everywhere. Anything a woman might want— from massage lotions and skin creams to shampoos and conditioners—lined the counter and thick white terry robes hung behind the door.

Jessica sunk lower and closed her eyes, allowing the water to lap her chin and physical bliss to envelop her.

But a sound at the suite door shattered her peace.

She sat bolt upright, heart slamming. Then she heard it again. Someone was rattling the door handle, trying to get in.

Jessica quietly got out of the tub, dripping water across the floor as she reached for the robe behind the door.

She pulled it on and, reaching for Luke's gun, she opened the door a small crack, heart pounding. She saw nothing.

Grasping the weapon in both hands now, Jessica edged the door open a little farther, and her heart stalled.

A man with pitch-black hair, black pants, and a long wool coat was bending over something on the coffee table.

Jessica raised the pistol, momentarily unsure whether she should fire at his leg or if she should aim to kill.

But the split second of indecision cost her.

He whirled round as he sensed her presence, lunging for her

before she could even blink. He slammed into her with the full force of his might, pinning her arms behind her in a steel grip as the gun clattered to the floor and her robe flew open, leaving her exposed down the front.

Jessica opened her mouth to scream, but he clamped the palm of his hand down hard over her mouth, forcing the terrified sound to die in her throat.

Chapter 12

"Why in hell did you sneak up on me like that!" His fingers dug into her arm as his eyes narrowed to fierce silver slivers. "I could have hurt you, dammit!"

She blinked in surprise, then stared. *"Luke?"*

His hair had been dyed pitch-black, his eyes startlingly pale in contrast. He looked like a stranger. Lethal.

Jessica's mind rocketed back to the night he'd grabbed her outside the phone booth and the same fear and uncertainty assailed her now. He really was a chameleon. She barely recognized him at all.

She tried to swallow, to absorb what stood before her, her heart still slamming against her rib cage. His coat was wool and fell to his calves, his shirt crisp white cotton, both designer cut. His pants were high-end as well.

He looked wealthy, urbane, but no less powerful.

Just as he'd morphed from a homeless man hunched over a shopping cart into her renegade savior, he'd shifted shape again.

"You…look so different," she said, her voice still hoarse with shock. "What happened to your hair?"

"I did it in the department store washroom," he said, his eyes drifted down to her exposed wet breasts, her belly. They darkened as they came to rest on the dark delta between her thighs. He swallowed hard and looked back up into her eyes as he slowly released his grip on her arm. He was breathing heavily. So was she. The sudden mutual sexual attraction spiked with adrenaline surged hot and fast between them, tightening her nipples.

She covered her wet body, quickly belting the robe. "You could have warned me it was you. Why on earth did you sneak into the suite like that?"

He said nothing, dark energy continuing to pulse around him, his eyes inscrutable

"Luke?" She cinched her belt tighter.

"I'm sorry I scared you, Jess." His voice was thick, rough. He bent down to retrieve his gun and checked the safety. "You startled me, coming from behind like that." He slid his weapon into his holster as he spoke. "Are you okay?"

She ran a hand through her hair. "I'm fine. I could have killed you."

"I don't think so."

"Oh, you're that sure of yourself, are you?"

"I'm trained, Jess. You're not," he said as he visibly gathered himself, removing his coat and tossing it over a chair.

"Well, I sure wouldn't like to be on the wrong side of *you* in a dark alley," she said. "Especially with that hair. It makes you look…dangerous. I didn't expect you back so soon." She hesitated. "What's in the bags?"

"Clothes for you," he said as her opened one of the packets they'd brought from Squamish. He took out a pair of scissors, along with a box of hair bleach and another box of platinum-blond hair color. "And we're going to have to cut your hair, Jess. It's too distinctive."

Jessica touched her hair nervously, her memory spiraling

back three years, to when they'd had to cut it all off after her abduction. She'd purposefully worn it as long as she possibly could ever since it started to grow back. She'd piled it on top of her head for her bath, but it had fallen loose in the tussle she'd just had with Luke, and it now hung in a curtain down her back.

She felt oddly vulnerable at the thought of cutting it off. As if she'd just reached some sort of crossroads.

"We better get started on your hair before anyone in this hotel sees it that way. We can order up some food after."

She moistened her lips as he advanced with the shears. "You mean right now?"

"Yes." He handed her the scissors and the boxes of dye. She looked at them. She'd never bleached her hair before.

"Jess?"

She glanced up.

"You okay with this?"

Moisture flooded into her eyes. She bit her lip, and nodded. "Yeah. I'm fine."

He hesitated. "Would you like me to help you?"

Inexplicably the tears surged down her cheeks. She nodded, struggling with her odd burst of emotion. "Thank you."

Luke stood behind Jessica, facing the huge mirror above the bathroom countertop, their reflection bouncing off it to reflect over and over again from the other mirrors that surrounded the walls. Her exotic whiskey eyes caught his in the reflection, showing an emotion he couldn't quite fathom.

He lifted the scissors, taking a handful of long silken hair in hand, his heart wrenching. He caught the lock between the scissor blades, and she braced, shutting her eyes.

But damned if he could go through with it and actually make that first cut. "It's a sin to cut this hair," he mumbled.

"Do it, Luke." The hard edge in her voice startled him.

He hesitated.

She grabbed the scissors from his hand. "You know what's

a sin? What those men have done to us. And they'll continue hurting people just like us on a much larger scale if we let them get away with it!" She grabbed a hunk of her own hair, thrust the blades into it, and hacked violently as a tears spilled down her cheeks.

Luke watched dumbfounded as a bolt of dark hair fell to his feet. He looked back up into her eyes. She smudged the tears away, and shoved the shears back into his hand, her mouth tight. "Do it. I can't see the back." Her pulse throbbed angrily at her neck right near her pendant, making it catch the light.

Luke blew out a breath, lifted the scissors and cut the rest of her hair off at shoulder level, the heavy tresses knocking softly against his pant legs as they tumbled to the floor. She kept her eyes closed, both hands pressed firmly to the counter in front of her, her body stiff.

"I want to be like my mother," she said suddenly, her words barely perceptible. "She never let anything break her. Not my dad. Not poverty. Nothing. She taught me everything I need to know in life."

Luke's throat closed in on itself. He steeled his jaw, cut again. Higher this time, his heart beating harder with each slice into the sleek dark curtain. He couldn't begin to articulate what this woman was doing to him. She was tearing him apart inside, making him feel things so deeply it hurt.

He really hadn't wanted to touch her again because he was afraid of the sexual power she had over him, the way she could snap his control.

He'd come completely undone again at the sight of her wet, bare breasts a few seconds ago. He'd wanted to take her right there on the carpet. Hard and fast.

He wanted to do it now.

He shifted on his feet as his body turned hot and firm with desire, backing away from her slightly lest she feel his arousal. The last thing Jess needed now was to feel threatened in any way.

He focused instead on watching her dark lashes flutter slightly each time he made another cut.

Her eyes flared open suddenly and snared his in the mirror, as if she'd sensed the sexual intensity of his gaze. Luke swallowed, caught off guard. The arousal etched into his features was blatantly obvious and he saw her eyes darken in response as she became aware of it. Luke could also see the pulse at her neck beginning to race.

"There." He lowered the scissors slowly, his voice turning thick and husky. "Looks pretty good, if I say so myself. Kind of untidy, but in a sexy way."

She didn't respond. Her exotic eyes turned mystically sensual as they continued to hold his steadily in the mirror, and her lips parted slightly, her breathing becoming lighter. Luke felt the blood drain from his head and flow south. He needed to get out of this bathroom.

But before he could move, she reached behind her and grasped his holster buckle, the movement making her robe spill open again, exposing her all the way down to the dark triangle between her thighs.

Luke's mouth went bone dry.

Wordlessly, she undid the buckle and slid his holster off, placing it and his gun on the counter in front of her. Then she unzipped his pants, hands working behind her while she watched his eyes in the mirror. Her dusky brown nipples peaked to sharp points and her abdomen rose and fell softly as she began to breathe more heavily. Luke could see the shift in his own face as desire consumed him.

Her hands found him inside his pants and he swelled into her soft palms. A smile played on her lips as she began to massage him and Luke thought his eyes might just roll right back into his head.

Then she turned slowly to face him, letting her robe slide right off her shoulders until it pooled at her feet and she stood completely naked in front of him. In the mirror, Luke could see the elegant line of her spine tracking all the way down to the swell of her naked buttocks. The visual effect of both a full-frontal and a rear view was overwhelmingly intoxicating.

Silently, she lowered his pants over his hips, crouching down to her knees as she did, her lips feathering his skin softly as she worked her way down his legs. As he stepped out of his pants, she placed her palms on either side of his thighs and, holding him steady, she began to tease him with the tip of her tongue.

Luke's limbs began to tremble. She reached for the bottle of massage oil on the counter, pumped a spurt of gold liquid into her hand and began to rub her palms together fast, heating the oil. Her eyes watched his as she did, and Luke began to throb so hard it hurt.

She stood slowly and, facing him, she took hold of his erection, sliding her hands softly down the length of his shaft right to the base. She cupped him there gently, and Luke's legs went weak as sensation speared through him.

She closed her hands gently around his shaft, pulling up slowly, before sliding them quickly back down. Luke heard himself groan as her slick, warm, oiled palms began working in rhythmic alternating movements until his entire body began to shake with the restraint of not grabbing her hips and thrusting himself deep into her.

She was getting turned on by his response, her mouth open slightly, her lips swollen, her eyes sultry and her lids lowering as she worked on him until he began to throb so painfully he almost released. He grabbed her wrists suddenly, halting her, and he moved her hands to her back. Then he lifted her hips and set her bottom on the cool bathroom countertop. Watching her eyes, he placed his hands on the insides of her knees and opened her legs wide. Luke could see she was ready for him and he could barely breathe.

But as he positioned himself between her legs, she placed her palms flat on his chest, stopping him. He saw what she was doing. She wanted to go slow and it was killing him.

He watched her hands as she took hold of him again, guiding the tip of his oiled erection toward the slick darkness between her open thighs. Hot skin touched skin and Luke caught his breath. She slid the tip in just so that it rested between her folds and she cupped the back of his head, gently bringing his mouth down to hers. Luke trembled with restraint as he kissed her with slow, drugging kisses, trailing his lips down her neck and along her breasts to her hard nipples. He sucked, flicked his tongue around them, teasing, biting softly, licking until he could literally feel the heat pooling around him between her thighs and she began to shake with need.

She suddenly hooked one ankle hard around the back of his leg, and yanked him close as she pulled herself up and slid herself onto his shaft like a hot, wet glove.

"Luke," she whispered, breathless against his mouth as he filled her. He lifted her buttocks, withdrawing smoothly, and thrust again, up into her slick, welcoming folds with one violent stoke, catching her body to his as her eyes went wide and black. She threw back her head and came immediately with a sharp cry.

Luke watched himself take her in the mirror, fast and hard, pushing farther and deeper into her as she continued to come again and again in the most intense, satisfying sexual experience of his life.

Still flushed and naked, they worked in front of the mirror to dye Jess's new short hair platinum-blond.

They worked in complete silence, nothing to hide between the two of them anymore, yet the sense of foreboding, of possible loss, lingered darkly over them.

They had their dinner delivered and they ate it in front of the fire wrapped in robes as they waited for the dye to take. Jess rinsed the color out in the shower and Luke stood behind her now, drying her hair.

It made him think of tomorrows. Of how he should never have gone this far with her. A sickening guilt welled up inside him.

He lowered the hair dryer. "Jess—"

"I know what you're going to say, Luke—I can see it in your eyes. But you don't owe me anything."

She turned to face him. "It's not like I didn't know the stakes. We're in this together. It's my choice." She ran her fingertips softly over his lips. "Besides, I was the one who got us—who got you—into this mess, not the other way round." She cupped the side of his face with her hand. "If it wasn't for me, Luke, you'd still be safe in your boathouse."

And alone.

It hit him right there—just how far he had traveled with her. He no longer *wanted* to be alone. And that was a first for Luke Stone.

Suddenly he grabbed her, kissed her hard. He wanted to say he loved her. That he needed her in his life. Always. That he couldn't imagine a future without her.

But he couldn't say it.

Not until she was safe. And that alone would destroy any hope of a future for them if it meant forcing her into a protection program, letting her go forever.

Desperation burned inside him.

There *was* one other way. It was foolhardy. Dangerous. Illegal. And it could cost them both everything.

But a surefire way to end a mob contract on your life was to kill the boss who had ordered it. The Dragon Heads operated under a set of near-religious codes, some dating back to the early Chinese imperial dynasties, when they were still a political force. One of those codes decreed that should the man who had ordered your execution die first, the order became void.

This was not feasible—certainly not under the banner of the FDS and certainly not in a country like Canada. The FDS operated in some real gray territory in lawless third-world locales, but a cold-blooded assassination carried out by an FDS operative on North America turf would kill Jacques Sauvage's hard-won United Nation's recognition for private military companies like the FDS.

If he got caught.

Luke might conceivably convince Jacques to condone the move, but the FDS could not sanction it officially. Luke would first have to sever any overt allegiance to the FDS. And if he got caught, he'd be on his own.

He could do it.

He could force himself to kill in cold blood for Jess. But there was one small snag—he wasn't sure if it was Xiang-Li he needed to take out or someone higher up.

Jessica dressed in sleek black designer slacks and a soft cashmere sweater that hugged her curves sinfully. Even the lace underwear Luke had bought her fit like a glove.

She leaned forward over the counter and applied some of the dark eyeliner and mascara he'd given her, but she left her lips nude with a mere sweep of gloss. The overall result startled even her. Her hair was roughly cut and very short. Tousled, it worked well with the platinum color, giving her an urban-chic, artistic, somewhat irreverent air. It accentuated the line of her neck and the color actually worked with her skin tone.

She'd stand out in a crowd, Jessica thought as she appraised herself in the mirror. But she could see Luke's logic—no one in their wildest dreams would expect the woman looking back at her in the mirror to be Jessica Chan, on the run from the triad after harrowing days of sheer terror.

She dared to smile at herself and it lightened her eyes, the dark mascara really setting them off. Wickedly sexy, she decided with a rare self-indulgent grin. And sophisticated, to boot.

And she walked into the living room with the confidence of a woman who knew she looked damn fine.

Luke was sitting next to the fire, working on his laptop. His eyes shot up when she walked in and the range of emotions that crossed his face was priceless.

"Wow," he said.

She held her arms out, and turned once in a circle. "You like?"

He swallowed. "Yeah," his voice was low gravel again. "I like." A smile tugged at his lips. "A lot."

"How'd you get the size so perfect?"

"I have a good eye." He smiled. "And an even better subject." He nodded toward the table. "I poured you some wine. Hope you don't mind if I carry on here—I need to work on this."

She sat and reached for her glass. "What is that you're working on?"

He didn't look up as he clicked. "I've accessed my files on Vancouver's local triads and tongs. The data I was beginning to collect is stored in a secure FDS server offshore. Other operatives around the world have been adding intelligence to the database as it comes in. It's a fairly new setup and we're the first to be collating international data on Asian crime at this coordinated level."

"You're trying to determine who the Dragon Heads might be targeting for assassination?"

He nodded. "It looks like the Wang Tse Tong run by Vancouver electronics baron Jimmy Ho has been busy with some aggressive turf acquisition of their own. Ho's tong is unlike the Dragon Heads Triad in the sense that he has no allegiance to the Chinese mainland at all," Luke said, scrolling down the page.

"That makes sense, given the historic origins of tongs versus triads," Jessica said, taking a sip of her wine. "Tongs were formed in early immigrant Chinatown communities to support marginalized immigrants and Chinese businesses. Like the triads, they evolved into criminal organizations, but they were formed without clear political motive. But triads originated as a political resistance to the Manchu emperor of the Qing Dynasty."

"Exactly," Luke said, clicking open another file. "It says here that Jimmy Ho is a fourth generation Canadian and a pure capitalist. It appears his tong is divided into cells—" he glanced up "—now *this* is interesting. From the intel filed by my FDS counterparts in the U.S. over the past few weeks, it looks as though Jimmy Ho has been forming key business partnerships with most of the major U.S. tongs and triads across the country." He looked up. "Jess, do you realize what this means?"

"That the Jimmy Ho and his tong are a serious threat to the Chinese Communist Party Dragon Heads."

"Exactly."

"Would you like some wine, Luke?" she asked, as she topped her glass up.

"No," he said, turning his attention back to his computer.

She stilled. "Luke?"

He glanced up.

"Do you have an issue with alcohol?" she asked, looking him straight in the eye.

His cool gray eyes narrowed, held hers. Silence consumed the room.

"I had a problem once," he said, finally. "For about a year after Rebecca's death. I have a close to photographic memory, Jess, and I was haunted by visceral images of her death, the blood, the tiny baby—my son—still attached to the cord. The smell, the slashes over her body and stomach, the sheer brutality of her death—it just wouldn't go away. And I hated myself." He inhaled deeply. "Guilt, remorse, self-loathing—you name it, I had it, and it ate me from the inside out. Scotch helped dull the edge. And I began to need more and more to keep myself numb. I guess I was kind of surprised I actually kept waking up alive each day. I hoped it would kill me. But it didn't."

"What changed?"

He rubbed his brow. "I met Jacques Sauvage. Actually, he came looking for me, hauled me out of a bar in Alice Springs. It's a long story, but he'd heard of my reputation and he was looking for someone with my expertise in Asian crime plus the covert special-ops stuff. His company is growing fast and he's always looking to recruit a good fit."

"Had no one tried to pull you out before Jacques got to you?"

He snorted. "Plenty. But it was Sauvage who spoke my language. Us guys from the FDS, we're all the same. Most of them are ex-French Foreign Legion, and they got there the hard way. Most went into the Legion looking for another chance, another life. A new name and identity. Under Sauvage's leadership, they come together in an unrivalled cohesive force. Sauvage is really a tough-love kind of guy—he's the glue that holds us together."

"So you stopped drinking?"

"Yes."

Jessica hesitated, recalling how he'd grabbed the whisky flask from her hand as if to prove something—perhaps to convince her, or even himself, that he didn't have a problem, that he could drink without sliding all the way into oblivion again. But he'd stopped himself before taking a sip.

Just as he'd tried to stop himself from sleeping with her.

The man was afraid of losing control because he didn't yet know what lay one the other side. She had to show him it was okay, that he had something to live for.

But then she remembered what he had said on the ridge.

"If you weren't going to disappear, this would never have happened."

"Luke, when we were up on that ridge in the snowmobile, you said—"

His computer beeped as a communication came through, and Luke held up his hand to silence her as he opened the file. He read it, his body tensing.

He quickly clicked on another file, studied it in silence, then whistled softly. "You need to see this, Jess."

Chapter 13

"That's my *father*," she said, going cold as she peered over Luke's shoulder at the old news photo displayed on his monitor.

"Taken five years ago while he was still consul-general for Britain," said Luke. "At one of Xiang-Li's Hong Kong casinos."

"So? That doesn't mean anything."

"Look over there." Luke pointed to two people in the background. "See that woman and that guy at the table with her? Do you recognize them?"

Jessica squinted. "No. The image isn't very clear."

"FDS techs enhanced this, Jess. According to them, that guy is Ben Woo, taken before he came to work for the Chinese consul-general's office in San Francisco—the same man you saw in that limo in Chinatown a few days ago."

Jessica rubbed her arms, suddenly chilled despite the roaring fire. "Who is the woman?"

His eyes held hers steadily. "Shan Huang. Now Shan Weston, wife of CIA director Blake Weston."

Jessica's mind reeled. She began to pace, her heart rushing

with that old thrill she got when she sensed a major story. She stopped suddenly, faced him.

"Luke, it doesn't necessarily mean anything. My father moved in diplomatic circles and Ben Woo is an assistant to the deputy consul-general. Woo had to have moved in the same circles back then, which meant he might well have known my father in Hong Kong. And Shan Weston has worked as a Chinese translator for the diplomatic service for years. She moved in the same environment as both of them. That doesn't mean she's on the side of the communist government. She's a third generation American citizen, for goodness sakes. A Yale graduate. I read about her in the papers when Blake was named director." Jessica paused. "The CIA must have checked her out when they appointed him, Luke. And just because Archer Stonaway was in a Xiang-Li casino doesn't mean he is connected with organized crime. Many functions of all persuasions have been hosted in Hong Kong casinos and, as you said yourself, you'd be hard-pressed to find one that isn't beholden to Xiang-Li in some way."

A part of her still did not want her father to be involved, although she couldn't for the life of her say why. Deep down, a part of Jessica wanted Archer Stonaway to be a great man who would acknowledge *her* for doing great things.

She ran her hands through her hair, momentarily startled to find it so short. She was being pathetic. Life didn't have fairy-tale endings, no matter how she'd dreamed of them as a little girl in London's Chinatown while her mother worked late at night.

Luke was studying her intently. "You're right, Jess," he said slowly. "None of it proves anything at all, but you add it up in a certain way and you've got something you can't ignore."

He stood, came to her, took both her hands in his. "What you've got is what appears to be international political corruption that goes all the way up to the top of the CIA."

He drew her closer. "Jacques's e-mail says the FDS is now running an extensive background investigation on both the Westons and Archer Stonaway. We'll know more soon. But

Jess," he said lifting her chin. "It's possible your father is tight with the Dragon Heads syndicate and has been for some years. This goes deep, much deeper than we probably realize." He paused, searching her eyes.

She felt suddenly adrift in her perceptions of who she was. "I…this is so weird, Luke. To think that my father is somehow behind my problems is…it's absurd. I just can't believe it."

"No, it's not absurd. I think Archer Stonaway's connection is the very reason you're still alive today, Jess. I think the Dragon Heads didn't hunt you down and kill you after your escape in Hubei because you *are* the daughter of Archer Stonaway—a man who is part of their organization."

"You're saying *he* stepped in and stopped them from killing me?"

"I told you, the Dragon Heads codes are ancient and fierce. Protection of members' wives, mistresses and children—as long as they remain innocent—is writ in stone."

"For that to be true, Luke, my father would have had to have acknowledged my existence."

"I believe he did."

Her eyes flashed wide. "You think he's actually known about me all this time? My job, who I am, what I became?"

"How could he not? You were a high-profile British media personality in China. He was a British consul-general to Hong Kong, China. This is a man who paid off—and threatened—his Chinese mistress to keep her from coming forward and making claims on him, remember? Believe me, Archer Stonaway is the kind of man who would want to keep sharp tabs on his ex and her child, just in case they ever became a threat to him and his career."

"I…" She withdrew her hands from his and stepped away, feeling suddenly small and insecure, as if the child within her had surfaced. "I…think I talked myself into believing Archer *didn't* know who I was, because it made his rejection somehow easier. But—" She looked up. "I don't know which is worse, Archer not coming to my defense and publicly acknowledging

I am his daughter, or my knowing he could be part of a major criminal network."

"He *did* acknowledge you, Jess. To the Dragon Heads. It's the only rational explanation for why they never came after you in England." He paused. "Archer Stonaway may have been threatened by the mistakes he made in his life, including you, but it was not in him to have you killed. I think he stepped forward when he had to and he took great risk in doing so. He did it for you, Jess."

"Great," she muttered as she went to the window and stared out over the city.

Luke came up behind her, ran his hands down her arms. He felt so good, so solid at her back. Luke was all she had right now.

He was all that stood between her and the world out there and she felt ridiculously vulnerable because of it—in more ways than one. She leaned against him and he nestled his cheek against her hair. Affection blossomed through Jessica's chest, and burned into her eyes. "So why can't Archer stop them now?" she asked softly. "Why is he letting them come after me?"

"Because you are no longer innocent, Jess," he whispered against her hair. "When you took those photographs, his pact with the Dragon Heads would have immediately been over."

She nodded. It made sense. She'd become a personal threat to the organization.

"You actually think Shan Weston is somehow involved in what's happening now, that she's a spy?"

"Could be more serious than that," he murmured into her hair.

She whirled to face him. "You mean Blake Weston *himself*? What on earth makes you think that?"

Luke inhaled deeply. "The way our movements have been compromised every step of the way over the last few days. And Shan links him straight to Hong Long, to Xiang-Li, to Ben Woo and, by default, to a Chinese government assassin. Those are serious connections, Jess."

"It could be Shan leaking his information."

"Then he'd have to be telling her everything about his highly covert ops, every step of the way. It would still be treason."

"She could be tapping into his communication without his knowledge, Luke."

"You think like an investigative reporter," he said with a grim smile. "Whatever is going down, it's going to rock the intelligence community one way or another and it's going to send the White House scrambling." He bent down and brushed his lips lightly over hers. "I have a call to make. Why don't you go get ready for bed. It's late, and we have an early start tomorrow."

"Meaning?"

"I'll explain later." He hesitated. "Which room would you like?"

She returned his gaze steadily. "Whichever one you're taking."

"You thinking what I'm thinking?" Luke asked Jacques Sauvage on his sat phone as he studied the images of Shan on his laptop.

"That Weston is our leak?" Jacques swore. "I hate to even think it, but it's the only thing adding up. It would explain what happened on our recent FDS mission in Ubasi."

"What *did* happen?"

"Five of Weston's men—deep-cover CIA operatives—were brutally murdered," said Jacques, his voice unusually grave. "It appeared a covert Chinese faction was working behind the scenes to undermine foreign oil interests in the Niger Delta, Ubasi in particular. And it looked as though a mole high up in the CIA had exposed the CIA officers working in the area by feeding intel to the Chinese."

"But nothing was proved?"

"No. All proof died when a convoy of mercenaries who might have given evidence was mysteriously attacked. Everyone, including the U.S. troops escorting them, was killed. The leads died right there. This could provide the answers."

"You mean Weston betrayed his *own men?*"

Jacques remained silent.

Luke's stomach felt tight. He swore softly. "This is big, Sauvage. This is going to rock the U.S."

"Never mind what it's going to do to international relations."

"We need more to go on. We need proof."

"We're working on it. The FDS has a contact who used to operate undercover for the Hong Kong secret police. He has access to law enforcement files that allegedly went missing years ago—files that never saw the light of day because of various criminal and political pressures. Our contact is checking those files for anything on Shan Huang's history in Hong Kong and on Weston himself. Weston used to be stationed in the East when he was still in the military. There's no guarantee our guy will find anything, but I'll keep you posted."

"In the meantime, I want to try something," said Luke. "If Weston bites, we'll know he's dirty."

"Shoot."

Luke quickly scrolled through a page on the Internet, clicked on a link advertising budget accommodation in Vancouver and explained his plan to Jacques.

Blake Weston felt ill. He'd heard nothing more from Jacques Sauvage since the chopper had been taken down by RPG fire. Now his paranoia was growing.

Sauvage might suspect something. Might even suspect *him*.

After all these years, this could all finally be coming to an end. He glanced at his wife.

Shan stood obscured by shadow next to a bookshelf in the library of their Virginia home, arms tightly folded over her waist, her skin ghostly pale. Even so, she was beautiful to Blake. She was quite literally his downfall.

His addiction. His weakness. There was nothing he wouldn't do for Shan. There was nothing he *hadn't* done.

The secure phone rang.

Blake shot another look at his wife, then grabbed it.

"Sauvage," Blake quickly pressed a button putting Jacques Sauvage on speakerphone. "What's going on? I haven't heard from you in hours." He tried to keep his voice level.

"The principal is safe."

Blake cursed silently. "That's the best news I've had all day. Where is she?"

"My operative has her under guard."

"I need a location, Sauvage. After what happened in Pemberton—"

"We have a leak, Weston, and it's not our end. The mole you have been trying to root out since Ubasi is someone in your immediate circle of confidantes and it's affecting our operations now. If it's any consolation, that narrows your search field considerably, but I cannot jeopardize my man and his principal. You have to plug that leak before I can divulge more information."

Blake swallowed hard. This wasn't all bad. Sauvage hadn't fingered *him* for the leak. "Look, the information will remain exclusively between you and me." Blake stole another look at Shan. "If you can give me a location, I can start thinking about moving men to a new pickup point while I look into our…other problem."

He heard Jacques Sauvage hesitate. "Fair enough. They're in Vancouver. This is the address—"

Blake closed his eyes as he listened, committing the address to memory, his heart racing.

He signed off and Shan stepped out of the shadow, her almond eyes focused intently on him.

"We have to make sure she doesn't talk, Blake. We'll lose our window. We'll lose everything."

"If we move on her now, Shan, the FDS will know for a fact I'm involved."

Shan's eyes held his steadily. "The alternative is worse."

Luke nudged Jessica gently awake.

She rolled over, opened her eyes sleepily. He felt his body stir in warm response. He smiled into her eyes. "Wake up," he whispered. "We've got work to do."

She squinted at the bedside clock. "It's four in the morning."

"Early bird catches the mole," he said with an affectionate prod to her ribs.

She laughed and hit him with the pillow. Luke caught the

pillow and stilled suddenly. She looked indescribably gorgeous naked in his bed, a tangle of white sheets low around her hips, short hair alluringly tousled.

Her eyes held his as unspoken meaning surged between them.

They both knew how much they had to lose now.

Luke said nothing, put the pillow down and quickly got up and went to get dressed.

The sky was black as they parked on a road above the Rosemont Motel in North Vancouver, near the docks. From their vantage point Luke watched through night-vision scopes as a soft mist descended on them in rolling clouds that drifted down the mountains behind them.

Two hours passed before there was any sign of movement.

He tensed as three dark vehicles pulled into the Rosemont parking lot. One parked in the front, the other two drove round the back.

Men dressed in black, with balaclavas, gloves and weapons circled round, making for the false room number Luke had taken from the accommodation page on the internet. Jacques had passed the information on to Weston who had assured the FDS it would go no further.

Luke lowered his scopes, anger simmering low in his gut. He'd seen enough. Blake was dirty.

He started the ignition, his mouth dry.

"What could you see?" Jessica asked quietly.

He steered the vehicle quietly into the deserted street, lights out. "I saw that it's the CIA director himself who wants you dead, Jess."

She swore softly. "But *why?*"

"Why would Weston sell himself out to the Chinese? Hell alone knows." Luke put on the wipers as the rain came down more heavily, the streets this side of the Burrard Inlet deserted at this early hour. He felt tired.

"I need to get you out of here, Jess. Before this blows."

"What do you mean?"

"I need to get you to São Diogo. Jacques said he'd have a Gulfstream waiting at Vancouver International. We're going straight there."

"No, Luke, wait." Tension rippled through her voice. "Just explain to me…what good would that do?"

"I can't keep you safe here on my own, Jess."

"What about *you?*"

He said nothing, hands tightening on the wheel, his chest constricting.

"You're supposed to get on that jet with me, aren't you?" she said very quietly. "That's what Jacques wants you to do. But you're not going to. Are you?"

"I need to do something first, Jess."

"Luke—you *can't* go after them. Not on your own."

"I can't run, either. Not anymore." He glanced at her. "You showed me that."

"And you expect *me* to run now?" she snapped. "Luke, just pull over and let me talk to you."

"I can't."

"Dammit, Luke! Stop, please. Talk to me! You at least owe me that."

He exhaled sharply, kept on driving.

"Please." Frustration choked her voice.

Luke was wrenched between heading directly to the Gulfstream and spending just a few more moments with Jessica.

He might never see her again once he put her on that jet. He gritted his teeth, his hands tense on the wheel. He pulled sharply into the parking lot of a take-out joint and came to a stop.

She exhaled deeply, scrubbed her hands over her face and looked up at him, exasperation gleaming in her eyes. His heart twisted and he looked away.

"Okay," she said. "This is how I see it. However this shakes out now, my testimony and photographs are going to play a pivotal role in exposing corruption in the Chinese government and the CIA. But if Xiang-Li and The Chemist are not taken into custody *right now,* while still on North American soil, they could slip back into China where it's going to be hard to touch them or even find them. Meanwhile, I'll go into a protection program and lose everything. And even then I'll still be looking over my shoulder every day, wondering if this is the day they come for me, because they will still be out there somewhere." She stared at her hands, and Luke realized she was shaking with adrenaline. "I *won't* live like that, Luke." She looked up into his eyes. "I won't get on that plane. The only way this is *ever* going to work out for me is if Xiang-Li and his men are taken down first."

"I know."

She stared at him in silence. "That's what you're going to do, isn't it?" she whispered. "You're going to try to find them yourself. You're going to try to kill them?"

"That wouldn't be legal."

"But that's not going to stop you, is it?"

He didn't reply.

"You can't do this, Luke. You'll end up behind bars or dead. It's not right."

"Nothing about this is right, Jess."

Her eyes filled with tears. "Please don't do this for me."

"Maybe I'm doing it for me."

She took his hands in hers. "Look at me, Luke, please. Let me stay with you. If you're going after them, then so am I."

His eyes locked onto hers, and his voice turned rough. "Jessica," he said slowly, his grip on her hands tightening. "I lost one woman I loved. I'm not going to lose another. This time, I'm going to do what's right."

The words knocked the breath right out of Jessica.

He loved her.

This one-woman guy who fell hard and forever had fallen for her.

Jessica couldn't breathe. Her eyes filled with emotion and her chest began to hurt. And now Luke was going to sacrifice himself to save her, the woman he loved. Just like he said he should have done with Rebecca, his wife.

She couldn't let it happen.

Jessica had finally found a man she could imagine spending the rest of her life with—a soul mate, a friend, an equal—someone to fill the emptiness that her life had become.

"I can't allow you do this, Luke," she said softly, tears threatening to spill from her eyes. "It's my fault you are in this situation. I'd rather die with you than live, knowing you died for me."

He closed his eyes briefly, steeling himself. And he shook his head. "My job is to protect you, Jess. And I will."

His phone beeped, suddenly, shocking them both.

He dragged his hand over his hair, and answered. "Yeah?" He sounded tired "Yes, the triad moved on the motel a few minutes ago. Affirmative, we're heading for the airport now."

He hung up and started the ignition without looking at her.

Tension whipped across Jessica's chest. "What was that?"

"Sauvage says the Gulfstream is fueled and ready to fly you to the Yukon where the FDS has arranged transport out the country via a military cargo plane bound for Russia. You'll avoid border issues that way."

He began to drive and panic slashed violently through Jessica. She'd found a man who loved her.

She loved him.

And it was over.

Chapter 14

Jessica had to do something—anything—to stop him forcing her onto that plane.

"You wouldn't have the guts to say you cared about me if I wasn't leaving!" she snapped in desperation.

"That is not true," he said, ramming the car into third gear.

"Yes it is. You slept with me because you knew you wouldn't have to commit."

"Oh, that's low." His voice had gone very quiet and dangerous.

"Oh, please. Don't deny it, Luke! You said it yourself. Up on that ridge on the snowmobile. This is very convenient for you. Put me on the plane and you're emotionally safe again."

His knuckles turned white on the wheel and his brow lowered. She was making him furious but she didn't care. She had mere minutes to change his mind and she was going to pull every trick out the bag, even if it meant hitting below the belt just to get a rise out of him.

"I've made the biggest commitment of my life right now, Jessica, by—"

"Oh, no." She shook her head, eyes burning, anxiety mounting as they neared the airport. "I'm not buying it, Luke. You're running again."

He was irate now. His eyes flared to hers. "You're making me angry, Jessica."

"Yeah? Well, I feel *betrayed,* Stone. You hand me over and you take away my one last shot at freedom, my last chance to buy back what the triad took from me, my credibility as a journalist. *Everything* that matters to me—" her voice hitched "—including you." Tears rolled freely down her face now, but she couldn't care less.

"Jessica—" he reached for her knee, but she pushed his hand away, turning to look out of the window at the dismal gray dawn behind rivulets of rain snaking over the passenger window.

He veered sharply off the road and screeched to a sudden stop. "What the hell do you want me to do?"

She swiveled round. "I want you to tell me how you're going to find Xiang-Li and The Chemist. I want to know what those men are planning to do in North America and I want you to help me stop them." She sniffed, angrily smearing emotion from one end of her face to the other. "And I want you to stop being such a bloody chauvinist, Luke Stone, and start treating me as your equal. We *shared* something, dammit! This is about *us!*"

An electrified tension mushroomed between them and they both sat in silence, humming with adrenaline as fine rain ticked against the roof and cars rushed by in the morning commute— a city going to work on a regular winter morning.

He suddenly shifted the car into gear and swerved back into the traffic.

She snapped alert. "Where are we going?"

"Back to the hotel." His tone was ice-cold.

A spurt of hot triumph shot through her belly. She swallowed, not daring to utter another word lest he change his mind before they got there. It was a start. A small one. And she was going to have to find a way to show him that he could not do this on his own. That he needed her.

That this was *their* battle. To fight as one.

"Can you get the pilot to stand-down?" Luke asked Sauvage on the sat phone as he clicked open his laptop files. He wanted to see if the FDS team had dug up anything new on Jimmy Ho and the Wang Tse Tong in the last few hours.

"Negative, Stone. We need you both out of there ASAP."

"Forty-eight hours—that's all I'm asking."

"Why?"

"Looks like we picked up a tail at the Rosemont," he lied. "I want to lay low until I'm sure."

Jacques was quiet for a moment. When he spoke his tone was ominous. "What are you up to, Stone?"

"Nothing." The Wang Tse Tong file opened on his laptop and Luke quickly began to scroll through the information that had been filed by the FDS techs overnight. If Jacques suspected he was going to go Rambo on him, he'd cut Luke's access to the central FDS databases. Luke needed to memorize what he could while he still had Sauvage on the blower.

"I'll have her there in forty-eight hours, max," he said, quickly opening another file, this one showing the passenger manifests the FDS had accessed for flights coming into Vancouver International over the past month. Luke's pulse quickened. He began to copy files over.

"I need you *both* on that plane, Stone. It's not our gig anymore, understand? We're trying to open a channel of communication with the White House."

Yeah, and that might be too late to get Xiang. "I gotcha, mate."

Sauvage hesitated, clearly not convinced. He knew his operative. "You blow this, Stone, and you don't have a future with the FDS—you do understand this?"

"Affirmative." Luke signed off and quickly hunkered over the files, tension whipping through his body. He didn't have a future anyway if he failed Jessica.

Because in failing her, he'd fail himself.

He was going to find a way to figure this out. But the biggest problem standing in his way was Jessica Chan herself. She was standing there right now, arms folded over her stomach, legs apart, glaring at him.

"What are you doing?" she said.

He slanted a look at her. *Feeling damn angry, that's what.* "I don't have time to talk." He turned back to files, copying whatever he could. Luke was betting Sauvage would terminate his access to the FDS mainframe within minutes, and justifiably so. The implication was that if Luke followed his boss's orders, he wasn't going to need this information, anyway. He'd be on a plane to the Yukon.

"Dammit, Luke. Let me in! Tell me what you're doing so I can help you."

"How?" he said as he copied another file.

"Tell me what you have in those files and *then* I'll tell you how."

He looked up, studied her carefully. Sparks flickered in her eyes, reminding him of an angry lioness, tail switching. She looked flat-out sexy and if he wasn't so gung ho on saving her damn life, he'd take her right there on the floor.

He turned back to his computer, and swore viciously as a red alert began to flash repeatedly over his screen. Access Denied. Access Denied. Access Denied.

"What is it?" she said, coming to his side.

"He shut me out."

"Well, now you know how it feels."

He snorted. "You're something else, you know that?"

"I wouldn't talk if I were you, Stone."

Luke grumbled a response, his attention suddenly riveted by what he was seeing in the passenger manifests he'd copied over. He scrolled through the lists, his pulse quickening with each consecutive page. The FDS techs had highlighted close to one hundred names and attached footnotes for each at the bottom of the pages.

He lurched to his feet, began pacing in front of the massive windows as morning lit the city now bustling below them. Clouds boiled down over the distant mountains, turning the sea a foreboding gunmetal gray.

"Talk to me, Luke. What did you see?"

He spun to face her. "Passenger manifests," he said. "Over the past two weeks almost one hundred influential Asian businessmen from across the United States have been flying into Vancouver."

Her eyes narrowed sharply. "What does that mean?"

"Those men, Jess, are not simple businessmen, they've been tagged by law enforcement across the country as organized crime heads in the U.S."

"You mean—"

"Not only that," he interrupted her, "but each and every one of the syndicates that those men are allegedly affiliated to has recently signed a memorandum of agreement with Jimmy Ho's Wang Tse Tong organization. They're all converging on Vancouver."

"Why?"

He dragged both hands over his hair. "I don't know. Maybe some mass tong gathering ordered by Jimmy Ho."

Jessica froze at Luke's use of the words *mass gathering*, her mind hurtling back to the Hubei factory warehouse where she was held prisoner.

"Luke?"

He stilled at the strange tone of her voice. "What is it, Jess?"

"The Chemist—his particular skill, the chemicals and biological tools he uses…they're for mass assassinations. Like the nerve gas he manufactured that killed those toy factory workers…." She rushed over and started rummaging through her clothes. "Damn," she said standing up. "Housekeeping must have taken it."

"Taken what?"

"The Chinese Independent Press newspaper. There was an editorial in there about a big business meeting up on Grouse Mountain—hosted and funded by ZEDEX Electronics."

"That's Jimmy Ho's company."

"I know! I didn't see the relevance until now. It's the first time the entire mountaintop venue has been booked for exclusive use, Luke. The article mentioned upward of four hundred guests and massive security measures, special Chinese chefs and staff for the occasion. It's apparently going to be some sort of an anniversary celebration."

"Or," he said, stepping closer to her, "the celebration of the birth of a super tong."

They stared at each other for a moment as the implications began to sink in.

"Think about it, Luke," she said. "A mass influx of pro-Wang Tse leaders, all potentially gathering in one contained environment, a killer in town who specializes in mass assassinations with chemicals that can't be traced—*that's* why Xiang and The Chemist are here. It's *got* to be!" Her eyes glittered with excitement and all Luke could think about was how much he loved this woman, how he'd love to spend the rest of his life on one big adventure with her.

He swallowed. He needed to focus. "And if Ben Woo is with them, it would mean the covert faction in Beijing is behind a mass assassination attempt," Luke said, pursing his lips as he considered possible scenarios. "If the Dragon Heads pull this off, Jess, it'll be like cutting off Jimmy Ho's multiheaded hydra in one fell swoop. Overnight, the Dragon Heads will take control of Asian organized crime on this continent. An assassination like this would spark fear into the hearts of any tong and triad member trying to contest this."

"The biggest criminal turf takeover in history," she said.

"Or is it a political one?"

"Maybe it's both."

He nodded, marveling at the sudden sexy spark in her eyes, thinking it was no wonder Jessica wanted her old job back. She thrived on it, just as he thrived on the adrenaline of his job. "It really is brilliant, Jess. But on the flip side, if this is what's going down, should the Dragon Heads miss this window, it'll be Jimmy Ho who retains hold on Asian organized crime on this continent. If we can stop that assassination, Jess, we can stop the Dragon Heads–Chinese Communist Party alliance penetrating the heart of U.S. and hitting where it hurts—the economy, the drug trade, biological weapons—you name it. When is this gathering supposed to take place?"

"That's the trouble, I don't remember. It was soon, maybe today—no, not today, today is the big day for Chinese New Year celebrations. Jimmy Ho wouldn't do it today. It could have been tomorrow. I had a sense reading the editorial that the party was supposed to happen before the week was out."

"That leaves only tomorrow or the next day." Luke came closer to her as he spoke. Simply incapable of resisting her simmering intensity, he took her face in both hands and kissed her hard on the mouth.

Her lips opened instantly, hotly under him. Lust and excitement surged through Luke as her tongue found his. But he pulled suddenly away. They didn't have time. "Call Grouse Mountain, Jess," he said, his voice husky. "Ask them about booking a dinner venue this week. See what you can find out."

She nodded, her eyes dark and gleaming from his kiss. "What are you going to do?"

"I'm going to go through the rest of these files, see if I can find anything else."

Luke had ordered breakfast, but apart from the tea and coffee, the food sat untouched on the table. "Okay," said Jessica, reading from her notes as she paced around the table. "ZEDEX Electronics has booked Grouse Mountain for tomorrow night. I got chatting with one of the lower level staffers at Grouse. When I asked for a dinner reservation, she said the mountain will be closed to the public because of the ZEDEX function. There will be about four hundred guests in total." Jessica reached for her coffee mug, took a sip. "The employee said most of the dignitaries—I'm presuming Jimmy Ho himself—will be flying in via chopper and using the helipad on top. The rest will upload via gondola. Only guests with passes and ID will be allowed into the gondolas and ZEDEX is providing its own security."

"Yeah, tong security. Automatic firepower to match," said Luke.

"Uploading will start around 5:00 p.m." Jessica looked up. "It'll be dark by then."

Luke nodded, checking the forecast on his computer as she spoke. "And snowing," he added. "Last of the back-to-back fronts will hit by tomorrow afternoon."

"The last gondola car will upload at 9:00 p.m. Once the party is over, they'll fire up the gondolas again and the guests will be downloaded while the bigwigs fly out on top."

"The employee told you all that?"

"She sounded young, excited by the whole thing. And I played along." Jessica angled her head. "I told you I always get the information I want, Stone."

He grinned. "I believe you." He got to his feet, poured some tea, and stood there holding his china cup and saucer like a rugged but suave James Bond with his black hair and ice eyes.

Jessica stared for a moment, wondering if he knew how truly gorgeous he was. A part of her could not believe she had found this man.

And that he loved her.

A chill sense of foreboding whispered through Jessica. It wasn't over.

She could still lose him.

They could both lose everything.

"It's perfect for a mass killing," she said as he sipped. "It's a contained venue. If they use a chemical or biological weapon, they'll kill everyone on site, no collateral damage. They send a real clear message as to the intended target this way."

"And because no one knows what The Chemist looks like, maybe he's found a way to get into the party himself."

"That's possible, perhaps with the aid of a traitor inside the Wang Tse. That's the way the Dragon Heads orchestrate their takeovers," said Luke. "They infiltrate first."

Jessica began to pace, the cold foreboding burrowing deeper into her. "Okay, if he gets inside, he'll want to administer a lethal agent that doesn't kill him as well. A gas would be out of the question because he'd need protective gear."

"Something in the food or drink, then."

She stilled. "That would be my guess, if he intends to walk away from this."

Luke took another sip of tea, watching her intently. "But if The Chemist does want to walk from this, he's going to need to get away before everyone dies and the police are alerted. And there will be no way off that mountain until the gondolas start up again. He'll be trapped."

"He could hike down."

"Not easy in this weather. People die up there every winter."

"Hmm." She tapped her pen on her notepad. "He could use a viral or bacterial agent that doesn't act right away. Instead, all the tong leaders ingest it, get infected, then go back to their respective cities. They die in their own beds across the country a couple of days later."

He stilled, teacup midair. "You're a genius, Jessica!"

She made a moue at him. "Told you I could help."

"Touché," he said with a grin. "And if they did it that way, their message would be even more effective—defy the Dragon Heads and they'll get you at home, right in your own bed. Terrorism at its finest."

She lowered her notepad. "We have to stop them, Luke."

He bit the inside of his cheek, nodded. "But how? Presuming we are even correct in our assumption."

"We could go to the police."

He shook his head. "We're wanted by the cops, remember? They'll tie us up in so much red tape it'll all be over before we can even talk."

"Anonymously?"

"And say what? There's going to be a mass killing on Grouse Mountain?"

"It's something."

He shook his head again. "I bet the RCMP are all over this gathering already. Those same names on the manifests that alerted the FDS researchers would have alerted them, too."

"Then the police will act."

"No, not unless they have something to go on. All it looks like at the moment is a massive clan gathering. They need evidence of something illegal."

"What about my photographs?"

"All they prove is that those men were seen in a town a few days ago. It says nothing about a mass assassination attempt. You know what we need to do? We need to get those images to Jimmy Ho. If he sees that Xiang is in town with an alleged assassin, he'll draw his own conclusions. The photographs will show him what The Chemist looks like, and blow any cover he might be using. Jimmy Ho can take his own evasive action."

"You're just going to pick up the phone and call Jimmy Ho?"

Luke chuckled. "I have no idea where to find him. Not without access to my databases. Calling ZEDEX cold won't help, either, given that it's Chinese New Year. No, we need another way to bring those photos to his attention before tomorrow afternoon."

"We could get them into the newspaper."

"No way, we'll never get a reporter to run with this stuff by press time tonight. They'd want to check facts—call everyone from the White House to Beijing to the RCMP. There's no time for that."

"Not the mainstream media, Luke," she said, stepping close to him. "The Chinese Independent Press."

"They'd want to check facts, too."

"Not necessarily," she said. "I've met the editor, and from our conversation about what happened to me in Hubei, I got the distinct sense he's not in favor of the current Chinese government. And if he's writing editorials about ZEDEX, I'd bet he is pro-Jimmy Ho and Wang Tse."

"Still doesn't mean he can just run with this stuff, Jess."

"Listen to me, Luke." She touched his arm and saw interest flicker sharply in his eyes again. "Some of those Chinese free press papers started as underground flyers aimed at protecting and informing disenfranchised Chinese immigrants. They were used as a political tool and that culture is still strongly ingrained." She held his eyes. "If we can impress upon the editor what it means to publish those photos by tomorrow morning, I think he'll do it. We could have a story and photos hitting Chinatown at the crack of dawn. Anyone in the Chinese community who attends the parade today will be picking up a copy tomorrow to see if their picture got in. The coverage will be massive and targeted exactly where we need it. The whole of Chinatown will be on the lookout for Xiang-Li and The Chemist. They'll have nowhere to hide. It could flush them right out into the open. Plus," she said, an edgy thrill mounting inside her, "the mainstream media will pick it up an run with it from there, reporting on the report."

Luke went silent, a dark sensual gleam in his eyes. "You truly are brilliant, Jessica Chan," he said, reaching for his wool coat and sunglasses. He shrugged into his coat as he copied files from his laptop onto a memory stick.

"What are you doing?"

"I'm going to Chinatown. I want you to wait here."

"Luke! Dammit! *Don't do this to me.*"

He strode to the door, coat billowing out behind him. "You'll be safer here, Jess."

She slapped her palm angrily against the door as he reached for the handle, blocking his exit. "Don't be an idiot, Stone. You *need* me."

"I need you here, Jess."

"No, you need me to speak Chinese. The editor doesn't speak English."

He hesitated.

"He knows me, Luke. He understands what I went through in Hubei at the hands of the Dragon Heads. He believed my version of the story and he's going to believe me when I show him those photographs—*my* photographs. Why should he believe you? He's going to run a mile if he sees you barging into his office looking like that."

"Like what?"

"Like some demon killer. Listen to me, Luke—"

"Jess, I can't risk putting you back on those Chinatown streets."

"The New Year's Parade starts in two hours. If we go down to the mall, pick up a few things for a costume, we can use the parade as cover. The parade route goes right past the newspaper offices, and we can just duck into the alley and up the back stairs. No one is going to see a thing. Plain sight, remember?"

"You *sure* this guy doesn't speak English?"

"Would I lie to you?"

His eyes narrowed. "I believe you would, Jessica, if it meant getting your way."

"Well, it's the truth, Luke," she said, her heart beating fast. "I've trusted you to this point. The least you can do is trust me now."

Jessica wore a curve-hugging red silk cheongsam that fell to her ankles with a slit all the way up to her creamy thigh. She'd put on his Ruby Passion lipstick and done some incredibly exotic thing to her face with traditional Chinese eye makeup and face powder.

Luke didn't know if it was the adrenaline pounding through his blood, or the cacophonous sound of pots banging combined with chaotic Chinese music, whirling dragons and costumed lions leaping for the lettuces being dangled off the historic balconies, but he didn't think he'd seen a woman more sexy in his life. He got hard just being next to her.

She'd kitted him out in an oriental black silk jacket with toggles and a mandarin collar, silk kung-fu pants and soft-soled kung-fu shoes. With his dark glasses he felt as though she'd dressed him for some foreign B-grade spy movie. "I feel like a bloody ninja on walkabout," he muttered against her ear as they ducked out of the colorful madness of the parade and hugged back against the brick wall of a dark, narrow alley.

"Ninjas are Japanese," she whispered, the sounds of the parade receding as it moved farther into Chinatown.

"I know that," he growled against her cheek. "Doesn't mean I don't feel like one."

She laughed, both nervous and exhilarated by the cold air, cacophonous excitement and by the sheer weight of what they were about to do.

They climbed the rusty fire escape of a heritage building and Luke jimmied a lock on the second floor, easing up an old sash window. They stepped into a deserted newsroom.

"The editor's office is at the far end, behind that door with the frosted glass panel," Jessica whispered.

Luke took her arm and led her through the desks. "You think he's even here?"

"He's got to be. The parade is big news. It's always in the papers the next day. The reporters and photographers will be out covering the event, but not him—he needs to get the layout ready for press."

Luke knocked once on the glass panel.

Chapter 15

They'd done it and both were high on adrenaline as they entered their hotel suite. Jessica and Luke had made it clear that the editor could face grave risk in publishing the photos, but he seemed so adamant in wanting to help that Jessica became convinced he was a solid Jimmy Ho and Wang Tse supporter, if not an active member himself.

"You think he'll be in real danger if he runs with it?" Jessica asked Luke, taking his hands in hers and walking backward as she led him into the bedroom.

"I think he's definitely a tong supporter," said Luke, eyes fixed steadily on hers. "If he is, he'll get tong protection."

The back of her legs bumped up against the bed and she lowered herself onto the cover, drawing him down onto her.

Luke's eyes turned predatory as he pushed her red silk dress up over her hips and hooked his fingers into her black lace panties, pulling them down. "Do you know what that Ruby Passion has been doing to me?" His voice was gruff, hungry.

She ran her tongue softly over her red lips. "Why don't you show me," she whispered as she opened her legs.

He slid into her, hot. Hard.

And they made love furiously, fast, fuelling the fire that already burned in them. Then they made love again later in the afternoon, ordered dinner, ate it, and spent the rest of the evening in bed. This time the edge was softer and their love-making gentle, slow and poignant. It filled Luke with a sense of bittersweetness. It made him afraid of the hollowness that would come with losing her.

He lay back and stared at the dark ceiling, listening to the faint wail of sirens in the city night. He didn't want this to end. He never wanted to leave her.

He thought about the Chinese New Year, how it represented the turnover in cycles, the coming of spring. How every member of that community cleaned house and started the new year with a fresh slate. That he and Jessica were on the cusp of the lunar year right now. And Luke's slate was far from clean.

He listened to Jessica's soft rhythmic breathing as she slept and he rolled over to watch her. His heart clenched.

He knew what he wanted now. He just didn't know if he could make it happen.

A pale gray dawn bled into the sky and Luke still hadn't slept a wink. He heard a soft thump outside their suite door. He jumped out of bed, grabbing a towel to wrap around his waist.

He'd asked the hotel to have the Chinese paper delivered to their door the minute it hit the streets. He checked the peephole, then opened the door and retrieved the paper. His heart thudded.

On the front page were pictures of the dragon and the parade. He flipped the paper open to page two, then three, then hurriedly flipped though the whole thing—no photo.

His chest went tight. He strode to the bedroom. "Jessica, wake up." He thrust the paper under he nose. "Read it to me. Did he write anything?"

She went silent, caught his eyes. "No photos?"

He shook his head. Jessica paled. She set the paper on the

bed and flicked through the pages quickly. Then again, more slowly, scanning each piece of editorial with her finger. She looked up and he could see fear in her eyes. "He didn't do it."

Luke lunged for the remote, clicked on the local twenty-four-hour television news. And froze.

The main story, just breaking now, was the ritualistic torture and death of the Chinese Independent Press editor, whose body was found in the Chinatown newspaper offices by a cleaner in the early hours of the morning.

Jessica covered her mouth as she stared at the TV in horror.

The television reporter was saying the editor had been stripped naked and systematically sliced to death "in a manner once used in public executions in late-Qing Dynasty China. The method is consistent with recent executions carried out by the Dragon Heads Triad, but this is the first time it has been seen in this province," she said.

Jessica's eyes shot to Luke. It was the way his wife had died.

He was standing still as a stone statue, remote still pointed at the television set, the look in his eyes murderous.

She felt sick.

"They got to him first." His voice was strange. "That's why the photo never got out."

"But *how?* And why would they kill him in such an overtly triad fashion if they wanted to stay under the radar?"

"Because he'd flushed them out, that's why," Luke said. "The editor probably called Jimmy Ho's people right after we left. My bet is the Wang Tse started going door to door and showing those photos around yesterday afternoon before they even had a chance to go to press."

"And word got to Xiang."

"And Xiang's people went straight for the editor."

Terror snaked through her stomach.

Luke threw the remote onto the bed, hauled out the suitcase he'd bought and began stomping about the room hurling her clothes into the case.

"Luke, what are you doing?"

"We're leaving. Now. Get dressed."

She sat up, holding the sheet over her breasts. "What good will that do?"

His movements were ferocious as he flung a blouse into the suitcase. "I told Jacques I'd have you on the plane in forty-eight hours—it'll still be waiting."

"Luke! Just stop a minute. What purpose is leaving going to serve? We have to find another way to stop whatever is going to happen on Grouse Mountain tonight. We *have* to go to the police."

"With what evidence? Our suspicions? I shot two men in Gastown, Jessica. I killed a few more in Pemberton. You killed a man, too. Five CIA operatives and a pilot died in that chopper. We go down for murder if we go waltzing into the cop shop."

He slammed the lid of the case down. "That editor," he said pointing at the television set, "was tortured, Jessica. Hell knows what else they got out of him. Most likely a description of you. Your identity. You said the editor knew your background, that he'd been following your story. If Xiang knows you're not running from him, but actively gunning for him, he's going to spare you no mercy, Jessica."

Her jaw tightened. "Put that suitcase down, Luke."

"Get dressed." He pulled on his shirt and jeans.

"I'm not leaving."

"You don't have a choice."

"I do."

"This is my gig, Jessica."

"No, it's mine. You're off the clock now, Stone. You said it yourself. You're not working for the FDS to protect me anymore. Blake Weston just wanted you guys to find me so that you could point him to where I was, and he could set the triad on me." Her eyes grew hot. She was terrified, but she wasn't going to get onto that plane and disappear, no matter what.

"They'll make you suffer like they did that editor, Jess. They'll slice you into little pieces like…like my…" He couldn't say it. "I can't let it happen."

"It's my choice, Luke. Not yours."

He stood rigid, shirt hanging open, exposing solid rippling muscle over his abs and chest. His jeans were slung low on his hips, the muscles at his neck corded. His eyes sharpened onto her like glinting knife blades. He lowered his voice, a menace creeping into it.

"It's got nothing to do with my job, Jessica," he said. "Now it's personal. I'm getting you out of this city, out of this province, off this damn continent. Whether you like it or not."

She met his piercing stare head-on. "If I don't stop those men, I'll never be free—at least not the kind of freedom worth living for."

"Look, we'll get Xiang. We'll get them all. *Later.* But right now you are moving. I'm going to check out of the hotel—don't want to send up premature red flags by ducking out. Be dressed by the time I get back."

"Luke!"

He was gone.

Jessica swore. She couldn't do this by herself. She couldn't force him to help her, either.

Desperation welled inside her and tears threatened as she reached for her clothes, but she froze when she heard him coming back. *He'd had a change of heart.* She yanked her sweater over her head as she rushed for the door. She swung it open…and four Asian men surged forward, backing her into the room. Jessica opened her mouth to scream.

It was too late.

She was struck across the mouth and hurled violently backward into the room. She thudded to the ground, banging her skull on the corner of the glass-topped coffee table.

The scream died in her throat.

And her world went black.

Having settled the hotel account, Luke signed off with Jacques and pocketed his sat phone as he watched the elevator lights wink steadily down to the ground floor. Jacques had assured him the jet would be ready and a flight plan filed for northern Canada.

The elevator stopped for a while on the third floor and Luke began to feel inexplicably tense. One step at a time, he thought to himself. She'd be safe on São Diogo. Where they'd go from there once this all hit the fan he had no idea. But at least she'd be alive.

The elevator dinged on the ground floor, and the doors opened. The instant Luke stepped inside he saw blood on the floor. A band of muscle strapped tight over his chest.

He crouched down, touched his finger to it. It was wet, warm. Fresh. A cold sensation crawled over his skin. He stood slowly, feeling for his pistol, unsheathing it from the holster as he glanced up at the roof. Nothing there.

The elevator stopped on his floor and Luke gently fingered the trigger of his Sig Sauer as the doors opened. He exited the elevator on the 20th floor, leading with his weapon. He saw no one in the corridor.

Their suite door at the end of the passage was closed, but something small and gold glinted on the carpet outside. Luke's pulse quickened as adrenaline dumped into his blood. He raced for the door.

He crouched down, lifted the chain, and the small Chinese characters spun in a little circle on the end of a broken link, making his stomach twist with fear. He clutched it fiercely in his fist, trying to control the violent wave of anger that surged through him. He stood slowly.

Weapon in position, he swiped the key card with his left hand, toed open the door and swung in full force, door crashing back, gun leading.

His heart stopped dead.

The floor was covered in blood. Tables and chairs had been overturned, a mirror smashed. Jessica's camera bag lay empty near the bathroom door, clothes strewn everywhere, his laptop gone.

Luke's stomach bottomed out.

He worked quickly through the rooms, heart pounding,

sweat beading. She was gone. They'd taken nothing else—just his laptop, her camera. And her.

Shaking inside, Luke crouched down and examined the blood. There was more on the table, along with a matted lock of platinum-blond hair—Jessica had hit her head, cut it open. His stomach lurched savagely

Luke closed his eyes for a minute, trying to stay in control, struggling to ward off visions of the blood his wife had spilled, of the baby. But he couldn't.

The memories crashed over him in a hot red tidal wave, churning the past into the present. He wanted to scream. He was a bloody fool to have left her alone.

He and Jessica must have been tailed from Chinatown. The editor himself could have asked someone to follow them on behalf of Jimmy Ho. And if the editor had found out where he and Jessica were staying, he might have given up that information during torture. An acrid taste filled Luke's mouth as he raced out into the corridor.

There was blood in the elevator, which meant they'd taken her down in it. He recalled it having stopped on the third floor. He jabbed the buttons, cursing. It was taking too long. He rushed for the fire escape, setting off the alarm as he flung open the door. The alarm hadn't gone off earlier, so he knew they definitely hadn't used the stairs. And they couldn't have exited via the lobby—they would have been noticed.

He burst through the fire door into the third floor corridor, and his heart sank instantly when he saw the big stainless steel service elevator. They could have used it to avoid the hotel reception area, but you needed a card to operate it.

Luke raced back into the stairwell, and down to the ground-level service entrance. He burst out of the building into cold winter air, grabbed a woman in hotel uniform as she pushed a laundry cart by him. "Did you see anyone!"

Her eyes widened in shock, and Luke tried to temper himself. "Did you see a blond woman come through here with some men?"

She looked worried, as if she was going to get in trouble.

"Please," he said, "it's urgent."

She swallowed. "They…said she was ill and they had to rush her to hospital." Her accent was thick French-Canadian. "I…I let them use the service elevator."

"Did you see which way they went, what kind of a vehicle they were driving?"

"No…I…I'm sorry."

Luke swore violently as he spun away from the woman and raked his hand through his hair. *Jessica was gone.*

And he had no clue where to even *start* looking for her.

He whirled on his heels and ran back into the hotel, hoping he'd find something—anything—in the room that might tell him where they had taken her.

Luke found nothing in the suite that could lead him to Jessica and his pulse began to race so fast he could barely breathe. He tried to click over into his Zen-like operational mode as he stared at the pool of congealing blood.

Jessica's blood.

He swayed slightly on his feet, and reached to steady himself on the bar. Something alien reared through him.

Panic.

This was the one thing he'd truly feared the most. *This* was why he'd never taken another close-protection job. Because he couldn't do it.

He'd failed.

Again.

They would kill her. Like they had massacred the editor. Like they had sliced his wife. They might be doing it right now. And he hadn't been able to stop it.

This was it—he was at the edge of his own terrible black abyss and he could feel himself tumbling over, completely losing self-control.

He sucked in air, braced his other hand on the bar and leaned forward, hanging his head down as he gritted his teeth and scrunched his eyes shut, trying to concentrate. But still the visceral images of his wife's death roared up from the black shadows of his mind, assaulting him, tearing into him, the sheer power taking him by surprise, melding the past into this very moment until Luke realized he was shaking violently, a red bloody rage clouding his vision.

He struggled to regain focus, to come up with a plan, but he couldn't even see, let alone think straight.

It was his fault. He'd been making love to her instead of moving her out, thinking with his libido instead of his damn brain!

His body acting apart from his mind, Luke reached for the bottle of whisky on the bar and took a solid swig in an effort to take the edge off so he could think again.

Bile rose in his stomach as the liquor hit. He winced and took another deep, long draft, seeing Jessica's leonine eyes in the gold color of the scotch.

Warmth kicked into his chest as the alcohol worked into his raging blood, and with it came the all-too-familiar creeping numbness as the vise of tension eased. A burn began behind Luke's eyes.

He hadn't cried for his wife. Or for his son.

He'd just got numb.

He'd gone and hidden at the bottom of a bloody bourbon bottle. He stared at the bottle in his hands, almost wondering how in hell it had got there.

Some old muscular memory, a dysfunctional survival habit, had kicked in, making him reach for that bottle. Jessica had broken his control and something insidious had taken over inside him.

Luke sank unsteadily down onto the sofa, the open bottle still in his hand, conflict twisting his insides. The sensation of the booze inside him was good, though. He'd forgotten just how fine it felt. He took another sip, swiped the back of his hand over his mouth. And the burn behind his eyes increased.

He couldn't do this.

He had to think.

He cursed violently, and hurled the bottle at the huge plate-glass window. Shatter marks chased outward from the point of impact as the bottle smashed and the yellow poison dribbled down the pane in oily rivulets.

Luke closed his eyes. And for the first time in four years he let the hot wetness of tears come, feeling the strange saltiness on his lips. He gave over to the emotion, just letting the foreign sensations assail him while he tried to gather what was left of his mind.

He had to find her. He'd had some kind of momentary and immobilizing meltdown, but *he* was in control here, not the goddamn bottle. And he was losing time.

He jerked to his feet, slightly unsteady.

The cops would be no help. The silence and fear that operated around Chinese gangs was notorious. The editor's murder would only compound that.

He needed to find Xiang-Li himself. If he could find Xiang, he'd find Jessica. He could run around Chinatown like a chicken without a head, chasing shadows—wasting precious time—or he could go direct to Grouse Mountain, where he believed everything would converge.

Luke just prayed Jessica would still be alive in a few hours.

He stared at the bottle, the broken glass, the reek of the liquor sickening now.

He *had* to believe she was alive. He had to have hope. She was a fighter. He'd seen that every step of the way.

Now he had to fight, too.

She was going to expect him to come for her and he wasn't going to let her down.

Luke calmed his mind, opening it to the adrenaline rushing through is blood, welcoming it, using it to beat back the blur of alcohol. And he went for his pack.

He still had his radio, scanner, Sig, spare cartridges, knife, night scopes, balaclava and flares he'd taken from the hunting cabin. He grabbed his jacket. He was going to get her. He was going to save her. And while he was at it, he was going to save himself.

One man against the triad.

And he was going in, guns blazing to hell. He was going to do what he'd been born to do. Protect the woman he loved.

Or die trying.

Chapter 16

It was dark; snow was falling heavily. RCMP vehicles lined the affluent neighborhood road that twisted up to Grouse Mountain, police maintaining a visible show of force yet staying well back from the actual base. They clearly knew this event was connected to organized crime, but had nothing to act on.

A helicopter thudded somewhere up in dense cloud. The RCMP had two response choppers of their own, pilots fully suited and on standby in a nearby school field, rotors turning slowly in the falling flakes.

Luke had seen the choppers as he'd cut through the forest on foot to avoid police detection. He'd parked about a mile away and was clad fully in black, complete with black balaclava. He was on a do-or-die mission now, not feeling the cold, aware of the falling snow only in context of logistics. He was focused solely on finding Jessica, doing whatever it took to save her.

He hunkered down in thickening snow between two parked vehicles in the lot at the base of Grouse Mountain and waited.

Although it was dark, the gondola cables were illuminated

by giant kleig lights that blazed from the operations station. The gondola building itself was a massive open-sided box, lofted about four-stories high. Luke studied the small glassed-in command center tucked at mid level. He could see one man inside, operating the gondolas. As one car went up, the other car simultaneously came down. Luke figured the cars had a capacity for about thirty people each.

Asians guarded the dock entrance and Luke had no doubt they were heavily armed under their long coats. The men had been checking the passes and IDs of each guest and staff member, matching them against photographs, then frisking them before allowing them into the enclosure. There was no way they'd have let Xiang-Li and The Chemist through if they had seen Jessica's photos.

He and Jessica had probably thwarted the plan thus far. But if Luke knew the Dragon Heads, they would not let this window pass. He had to operate on that assumption that they would still act with a plan B, and within in the next few hours.

But how? And where was Jessica?

The snowfall grew heavier, great swirling flakes in gusts of wind. A gondola whirred out of the dock and lifted majestically into the air. Luke checked his watch. That would be the last upload.

Time stretched, the whiteness lending a surreal and muted quality to the night. Luke could hear snatches of Chinese on the gusts of wind. He began to feel tense.

A dark SUV pulled slowly into the lot, tires crunching softly through fresh snow. It came to a stop around the side of the gondola building. Four men alighted. They ran in a crouch, flanking either side of the building.

Luke's pulse quickened. He drew his Sig, inched forward along the wheel hub, and peered around the fender, staying low.

The driver side door of the SUV opened and a man in a tailored black suit with a cravat got out and lit a cigarette, the light inside the vehicle going on momentarily. Luke's heart stopped. In that small instant, through the crack, he saw her. Jessica. Alive!

Bound and gagged. A bandage on her head. *Alive.*

The door shut.

Luke's chest cramped. He had to focus on the moment, not her. She was alive and that's all that mattered. He just had to keep it that way. He would be useless to them both if he lost his cool.

Why had they brought her here?

Luke inched out from his cover and ran in a crouch to the far side of the station, pressing back against the concrete wall. He checked his watch. The last RCMP patrol had been by two minutes ago. The cops had been cruising past the base every fifteen minutes. All would be quiet for a while if they kept that schedule.

With the last gondola having uploaded, Jimmy Ho's security personnel relaxed, several of them moving off the side and lighting cigarettes. That was shoddy, thought Luke. Never occupy your hands and never leave your station. It told him these guys were amateurs.

Because of it, they didn't see the four Dragon Heads emerging like black ghosts from the shadows. They leapt on Ho's security guards and Luke heard a quick succession of soft pops—bullets traveling through silencers—as the Wang Tse security guards were felled.

The Dragon Heads dragged the bodies swiftly down into the dark bay below ground level while one crept along the dock and shot through the lock of the door that led up to the gondola control booth. Within seconds, the operator had been shot and dragged quickly out of sight. An Asian positioned himself behind the controls wearing the operator's orange jacket and cap.

One of the men whistled—a signal. The door of SUV opened again and Jessica was bundled out. She staggered into the snow, hands bound behind her back. Luke's muscles compacted as he saw who was pushing her toward the gondola—Xiang-Li himself.

Behind him was the man Luke recognized from the photograph as The Chemist.

Luke's throat closed as he watched Jessica stumbling in front of the men. She was clearly injured and unsteady, her face white with fear, her eyes dark hollows.

Rage arrowed into Luke's heart, but he forced the emotion to a distance. *Focus.*

As she neared he saw she had some kind of apparatus strapped to her chest. It hit him then.

They were going to use Jessica to deliver the lethal agent in the form of a small detonating device strapped to her chest. It would kill her in the process—exacting revenge—and slay the tong heads at the same time. It would also allow Xiang and The Chemist to walk away undetected.

The plan had a distinct symmetry to it, thought Luke. He should have seen it coming.

Even if the Wang Tse guards shot her as the gondola docked on top of the mountain, it still wouldn't stop the device from exploding on her body, and releasing whatever toxin or biological agent was in there.

Luke did not have a moment to lose.

He ducked round the rear of the building and used a pole and tree to maneuver himself up to dock level. He climbed over the balustrade, pulled himself up onto the roof of the ticket booth, then swung up onto the railing at the control tower level.

Luke sneaked around the side of the booth, careful not to alert the triad members inside. Then he swung himself up into the metal rafting high above the dock, climbing out onto the iron maintenance ladder that angled over the gondola car.

Below him Xiang-Li forced Jessica into the docked car, tying her to the railing inside while The Chemist made his way up the stairs to the control booth.

Xiang-Li then joined The Chemist in the control station. Luke could now see all six men in the brightly lit booth. Just then, the bull wheel started to crank as the gondola doors swung shut and the car began to slide forward.

Adrenaline speared through Luke.

If he didn't reach her now, he would lose her forever. He swung himself round and dangled from the ladder by his hands until the car was almost below him. He dropped onto the gondola roof with a thud as the car moved into position under him, instantly flattening himself to the slick surface, planting his feet wide for purchase.

Squinting through falling snow, Luke aimed his Sig at the control booth as the car swung out of the bay. He focused on the centre of Xiang's forehead, and pulled the trigger. Glass shattered, and Xiang went down. The other men jerked instantly into action, returning fire.

Bullets hit the gondola as Luke fired again, the men easy targets in the brightly lit booth. He dropped the operator, then two more men as The Chemist fled for the back door. Just then the gondola swung into the full glare of the kleig lights, throwing a blazing spotlight onto Luke.

Immediately a bullet buzzed angrily past his ear. Then another, and he felt a jolt as something sliced into his upper arm. He bit down on the sensation, eyes watering, and fired again, felling the man who'd shot him, the distance between him and the booth increasing by the second as the gondola rose fast into the cloud.

The Chemist had the back door of the booth open, was almost out. Luke aimed carefully through the blowing snow. It was his last round. His last shot. He couldn't afford to miss. He depressed the trigger slowly and his bullet hit its target.

The man stiffened, turned. His eyes were the last thing Luke saw as the car was swallowed by dense cloud.

He had maybe fifteen minutes max before they reached the mountaintop. Luke reckoned it would be at least another ten minutes before the RCMP, out of earshot of the gunfire, drove by the station again and discovered the carnage—not soon enough to stop the gondola before it docked on top. He had to find a way to stop it himself.

Pain searing through his upper arm, hot blood wetting his clothes, Luke inched over the iced roof on his stomach, making for the side with the open window. The temperature plunged as they rapidly gained altitude, wind increasing as they neared midmountain, buffeting the car, causing Luke to slip as his fingers turned uncooperative with cold.

He edged his body over the side, his fingers gripping frozen metal, the only thing stopping a plunge into the void below. Luke steadied his breath, and maneuvered his legs cautiously through the narrow window.

He thudded down into the car.

Jessica struggled to jerk free when she saw him, her eyes glassy, her skin sheet-white. He tore off her gag. "Luke! Oh God, Luke, you've got to get out! I…I've got a bomb on me!"

"Jessica—" he grabbed her shoulders. "What have they strapped on you?"

"Please…go!" She was shaking violently, her skin cold as ice, tears and dried blood staining her face.

Luke struggled to compartmentalize his emotions. He took her face in both hands. "Focus, Jess, what have they done to you?"

"Please, you've got to get out of here." She was crying now.

He tightened his grip. "There's nowhere to go, Jessica."

"There is! Climb back out, go up that ladder, catch onto one of the pylons—" She saw the blood on him. *"Oh, God,"* she whispered. "You've been shot."

"It's nothing," he said, shouldering off his pack and digging for his flashlight. He aimed it at the apparatus wired to her chest, and his stomach turned to water. A small red light flashed next to a timer. It was definitely a bomb and it contained two sealed vials of liquid side by side.

His voice came out flat. "Do you know what's in the vials, Jessica?"

"It's…it's a gas. The same kind they tested on the Chinese factory workers. When the timer goes, a small detonator will rupture the glass seals and two chemicals will interact to form a lethal cloud," her voiced cracked. "I…I heard them say it has an instant kill radius of about five hundred yards before it starts dissipating."

Luke studied the apparatus, heart hammering. "The timer is set to go in twelve minutes—it'll blow as this car docks on top." He scrambled in his pack for his scanner and military radio, and quickly started searching for the police frequency.

"What are you doing?"

"Bringing in the cops."

"They'll charge you with murder, Luke."

"So be it." Luke found the channel, keyed his radio. He had less than twelve minutes to stop the woman he loved from becoming a living bomb that would kill hundreds of people—the biggest gang mass murder in recent history.

"*Mayday, Mayday,* can anybody hear me?" he shouted into the radio, opting for the universal call for help.

The radio crackled to life. Luke quickly told a dispatcher there was a chemical bomb on board the Grouse Mountain tram and it *had* to be halted before it got anywhere near the top.

He prayed the Mounties down below would get the message. If they were near the control booth, they might stop the tram in time.

He turned his attention back to the device strapped on Jessica, examining it with his flashlight. It was well beyond his technical expertise. There was no way to get a bomb tech up here and cutting the wires himself could set it off prematurely. He couldn't risk it. Yet.

"What else did they say about this gas, Jess. Did they say anything about skin contact?" he said, unsheathing his knife and severing the rope that bound her wrists to the railing. "Or is it lethal only by inhalation?"

"I…I think it's only inhalation," she said rubbing skin raw from the ropes. But please, Luke, there's no time. Save yourself."

"My job, Jess," he said very softly, "is to save *you*."

"You'll die."

He touched her tear-stained face. "Then we die together, okay?" The gondola jerked suddenly to stop and swayed in the wind. The radio crackled to life. It was the RCMP. They'd done it. They'd stopped the car.

Luke quickly explained the situation to an RCMP officer below, saying a nerve gas would release within ten minutes, and that police should evacuate the area below in case the wind carried some gas down. "I saw the choppers on the school field," Luke barked into the radio. "Are they equipped with first-responder hazmat kits?"

The cop said they were, as per the new regional policy.

"You've got gas masks?"

"Affirmative."

"And you're ready for liftoff?"

"Affirmative."

"Can you lower a kit via long-line?"

"We can try, if you can get up to the gondola cable."

"Do it. We're just north of tower thirteen. I'll shoot up a flare."

Luke scrabbled in his pack, finding the flares and the pen-size launcher he'd taken from the Pemberton hunting cabin. He loaded one and shot it through the window into the snowy night. It whooshed up, exploding into a luminous pink umbrella of light that hung above them. He now had less than ten minutes to get back onto the roof and climb to the top of the service ladder that led to the cable grips. He pushed the flares and launcher into Jessica's hands. "Shoot another one if that one dies out."

Wind whistled in cables high above him and the car swayed from side to side as Luke dragged himself up the ice-encrusted ladder using only one hand. His left arm was now useless, pain blurring his mind, but he held on. He held on to the promise of a tomorrow. A future. With Jessica.

If he couldn't do this—there wouldn't be one.

He reached the cable, dizzy, praying the RCMP helo would make it before he passed out from blood loss. He hooked his good arm through the cable and hung there. Way below him, the tips of giant snow-caked conifers were thrown into eerie relief by the pink light of the flare.

Another flared whooshed past Luke and popped into the sky, adding even more light. Smart girl, he thought. She was making damn sure that chopper would find them.

Then he heard it—the thudding of rotor blades in the cloud. Relief burned through him as the mechanical beast materialized above him, illuminating the gondola with a bright white spotlight.

The RCMP chopper lowered carefully, pummeling him with downdraft that ripped at his tenuous grip on frozen metal.

A kit swung down from a rope, secured by a grappling hook. But it swayed just beyond Luke's reach, the pilot risking his own life as he battled wind in an effort to bring it even lower. If the kit or rope snagged the gondola cables it would pluck the chopper right out the sky. Luke had to get higher.

He inched upward, hooking his legs around the cable and reaching precariously for the swinging first-responder kit with his good arm. He just managed to touch it with frozen fingertips, which forced it to swing out in a wild arc and slam back into his wounded shoulder. Luke stifled the primal scream that erupted from his lungs, eyes watering in pain.

The pilot made another pass, spotlight almost blinding Luke as he squinted up into the downdraft and driving snowflakes. This time he caught the case, unhooked it and signaled to the pilot. The chopper rose, disappearing into the cloud.

Luke looped the kit straps over his chest and slid down the ladder in a virtual freefall before bashing down onto the roof. He swallowed another bolt of pain.

Shaking, his vision blurring from exhaustion, muscles uncoordinated with hypothermia setting in, he inched over the roof toward the edge, aware of the long drop down.

Haste now would mean a slip and Jessica's death.

With seven minutes left, he carefully maneuvered the kit over the edge of the gondola, forcing it in through the window before squeezing in and thudding down behind it.

Jessica rushed to his side as Luke battled to open the first-responder kit with one hand, his face a sheen of sweat in spite of the cold. Jessica shoved his hands aside, quickly opened it herself, and extracted a gas mask.

Luke slumped back against the side of the gondola, weakening, his consciousness slipping. She attempted to hook the first gas mask over his head.

"No…you…first."

Her eyes just narrowed in defiance as she positioned the mask over his face and tightened the straps for him. Then she put one on herself.

Luke's vision blurred momentarily.

She grabbed his shoulders. "Are you okay?" Her voice came through the mask, distant and tinny. He met her eyes behind the visor and with Herculean effort, he pulled himself up and reached for his knife. The timer on her chest showed two minutes and counting down.

He inhaled deeply, feeling as though he was sucking air through a tube. "I'm going to cut it off, Jess." His voice sounded like an automaton's. "It's our only shot now. If it's booby trapped and goes, we pray the masks work. If it doesn't blow, we toss it and get lucky."

She nodded, eyes huge.

He peeled off his blood-soaked jacket, folded it into a thick pad and wedged it in under the device on her chest in the hopes that the detonation would be small enough to simply crack the vials and not hurt her. The jacket might help shield her from taking any direct impact in the chest.

Luke hooked his knife under the wires across her chest, and looked into her eyes, less than fifty seconds left.

"Ready?"

She nodded.

And he sliced through the wires. For an instant his heart clean stopped as they waited for the explosion. But nothing happened. Hot relief gushed through Luke as he struggled to get himself to the window and hurl the bomb out over the conifers.

He saw it tumble downward, then his body gave up, his vision narrowing to a small dot of light as he slumped heavily against Jessica.

As she helped lower him to the floor, they heard a soft and distant pop. Jessica scrambled across the floor, retrieved the flashlight and, shaking with adrenaline, she pointed it down into the snowy darkness. A faint yellow cloud drifted up among the snowflakes.

Fear whipped through her body. She sunk slowly back to the gondola floor.

"Gas?" he asked.

She nodded.

"We…wait it out. The cops know." She could hear him fading. "They'll have…hazmat team…coming in. They'll lower us down when…all clear."

"You need medical attention *now*, Luke."

He shook his head.

Jessica grabbed his knife and, using the blade, she cut back his shirt, locating his wound. With the aid of the flashlight she could see the bullet had tracked clean through the outer flesh of his upper arm, leaving a ragged trough of torn and bloody flesh.

She scrambled over to where the jacket he'd wadded up had fallen. She hacked at the jacket with the knife, quickly making wads to press into the wound and strips to bind them in place, wishing she'd concentrated in her high school first-aid class. All she knew was that pressure must be applied to the injury.

She scooted back over to him, pressed the wads tightly against the open flesh and used narrow strips to tightly bind the wads into place.

"Thank you," he whispered.

She snugged up against him and held him in her arms.

All they could do now was sit on the floor together and wait to see if they might die. Or if the gas masks would save them.

"Jess…" his voice was very weak now and a new kind of fear grabbed her by the throat.

"Luke, just hang in, please."

"We…did it, Jess."

A ball of emotion shot to her chest as it hit her—they really had done it. She'd seen Xiang-Li go down with her own eyes as Luke shot him from the roof above her. She'd seen him hit The Chemist, too.

They'd stopped global conspiracy and a mass murder.

For the first time in three years she dared begin to think she might finally have won.

Luke was watching her from behind the visor and Jessica could see the glimmer of tears in her man's eyes.

"I thought…I was going to…lose you. Fail. A…gain…I…"

His eyelids drooped and his voice drifted. She held him tighter. "Please, Luke, don't talk. Save your energy."

"If…the masks work, Jess…if we get down there, if we live…I'm going to marry you."

"What?"

"I'm…my…wife…" His eyes rolled back and his head slumped onto her shoulder, his weight suddenly dead-heavy against her. That same rock-hard body that had pinned her down in Blood Alley, that had come to her rescue over and over again, was suddenly limp and lifeless in her arms.

Desperation crashed through her.

He'd asked her to be his wife, to be with him *forever,* and he was sliding from her grasp right here, right now. *"Luke!"* She tried to shake him. She had no idea what to do. She couldn't remove his mask and try CPR—not with the gas cloud floating about. It would kill them both.

She scrambled over the floor, reached for the radio. She keyed the button, praying it was still tuned to the RCMP channel. "Hello! Hello! Can anybody hear me? This is Jessica Chan in the gondola. We need help, medical assistance ASAP. Got a man down. Luke Stone…he's…" her voice cracked.

"Ms Chan? This is Sergeant Ames of the RCMP, can you repeat, please?"

Relief gushed through her. She realized how distorted her voice must sound with the mask. She tried again, voicing the words clearly, slowly, her hands shaking. "Luke Stone has been shot. He needs medical attention at once. He's lost…a lot of blood…" tears began to choke her words. "He needs help. Please." *Before he dies. Before I lose the man I love. Please don't let this happen.* "Please. Can you hurry, Sergeant!"

"Ms Chan, we have a hazmat crew at the base of tower thirteen now. The air is beginning to read clear. It looks like most of the gas is dispersing in the wind, we'll bring you down as soon as we can."

She curled tight next to Luke and rubbed his arms. "Luke, stay with me. Please."

Chapter 17

Five days later. Lions Gate Hospital.

Luke opened his eyes, confusion swimming in his brain. Hospital—he was in a hospital. He tried to sit but couldn't. A wedge of worry rammed into him.

Then he saw her, her honey eyes softened with compassion. And love.

He relaxed slightly.

"Hey, it's okay," she said, placing a hand softly on his brow. "You're going to be fine." She smiled. "Thanks to about a gallon of new blood and antibiotics."

He held her in focus, just absorbing, trying to piece together time and events, but his memory was failing him.

She took his hand in hers, her skin warm and soft against his. "The doctors said you'd regain full use of that arm provided you follow the physiotherapy." She smiled again and it reached right into her whisky eyes. He just stared at her, his heart going light. She was wearing a soft pink cashmere sweater that skimmed her breasts and highlighted her lean waist. Her hair was tousled. Sexy. A hint of gloss on her lips. She was the most beautiful thing he'd ever seen.

"I have little doubt you'll beat yourself back into shape in superhuman time, Luke Stone."

He frowned as snippets of memory jumbled into his brain. "What…about—"

She leaned forward. "Xiang-Li died on scene at Grouse," she said quietly. "And The Chemist is in custody. He's permanently paralyzed, Luke." She glanced over her shoulder, making sure no hospital personnel were listening. "A bullet shattered his lower spine." She leaned even closer, lowering her voice. "They're not prosecuting anyone, Luke. They're not even acknowledging you shot him. Some deal has been worked out with the FDS, the Canadian authorities and the U.S. government. He's giving Blake Weston up. The CIA chief is going down. So is his wife."

Luke closed his eyes for a moment, trying to digest the fact they'd done it. They were finally free. A future ahead. His chest began to ache with the notion.

"Jacques Sauvage contacted me and filled me in with the details. He wants you to call him when you're feeling up to it."

His brow knitted in confusion again. "How did he contact you?"

She smiled. "I answered your phone."

"When did all this happen? How long have I been here?" Luke struggled to sit again as he spoke, pain tearing at his body as he did, making his eyes water. Jessica put her arms around him, helping him up, her breasts brushing softly against his chest, her breath sweet against his lips. All he wanted to do was kiss her.

She brushed back a lock of hair that had fallen over his brow, a hint of worry sifting into her eyes. "You've got to take it easy, Luke. You've been in and out of consciousness for almost a week. You developed septicemia. You're lucky to be alive."

"And your head—it's okay?"

She touched the small bandage on her temple. "It's fine."

"What did Sauvage say about the Westons?"

She sat on the edge of his bed and spoke very softly. "He told me Shan Weston had been recruited by the Chinese while still a student at Yale. Ben Woo was a foreign student at Yale at the time, working undercover for a hard-line arm of the Chinese Communist Party to target Americans of Chinese heritage for the creation of a U.S. sleeper cell. He'd found Shan—a third generation American of Chinese heritage—particularly receptive," said Jessica as she reached for a damp cloth, and wiped Luke's forehead again. "You're still running a fever, Luke. This can wait."

He shook his head. "I want to know. Now. All of it."

Jessica nodded. "Shan came from a cash-strapped background. Her grandfather was in desperate need of medical attention her family could not afford. She was disenchanted with U.S. capitalist policies and she was also keen to get in touch with her Chinese heritage, so she'd joined the Chinese Cultural Club at Yale, which is where Woo first approached her, offering to pay for her grandfather's medical costs in return for her loyalty. It apparently wasn't a tough decision for her."

"She's been working for the Chinese ever since?"

"Yes. As a sleeper at first. Then deep cover, working her way into diplomatic echelons as a very talented translator. Her job gave her reason to travel to China."

"How did she get to Blake?"

"When Blake was named potential CIA chief, Shan was sent to work on him. It appears the Chinese had already pegged him as a man with a voracious sexual appetite for Asian women. He'd demonstrated this while serving in the military, stationed near Hong Kong." Jessica removed the cloth from Luke's forehead. "You want some water?"

Luke shook his head. "Go on, please."

She moistened her lips. "Jacques's contact in Hong Kong came up with evidence contained in old secret police files—photographs of Blake in increasingly compromising positions with Asian prostitutes. The photos had been taken as part of a covert Chinese Communist Party campaign to target American servicemen and diplomats for potential bribery. They'd paid the prostitutes to work with hidden cameras and to be informers," she said.

"And they used these against Weston?"

She nodded. "Although use of prostitutes in itself was not necessarily incriminating, Blake's sexual appetites had grown progressively deviant over the years and the file on him had grown correspondingly fatter as his career climbed. It was this file that was the first tool of bribery Shan Huang first used on Blake, after she'd already seduced him into her own bed."

Luke smiled grimly. "Weston was doomed from the moment he met her."

"Yeah. He was. Shan was his type and she knew how to meet his…appetites. She aggressively encouraged him to gun for the top CIA job. Blake was appointed chief and as his pathological dependence on his wife grew, so did the scope of his intelligence transgressions."

"And with each transgression, the bribery potential grew correspondingly more severe, until Weston was irreversibly committed to a course of self-destruction."

"Exactly," said Jessica.

Luke struggled to sit a little higher, fast becoming frustrated with his injuries. "What I want to know, Jess," he said with a sharp grimace of pain. "Is how Weston knew you'd taken the photographs in Chinatown. Was there an informant in the RCMP?"

"No. Even though the Mounties told me to return with the developed proof, they nevertheless alerted CSIS, which has been cooperating closely with the CIA since 9/11. The information went straight to Weston. He instantly informed the triad, fearing photographic evidence of Ben Woo with Xiang-Li and The Chemist would prompt an investigation into Woo's background, which would in turn link Woo to Shan and lead to Weston's own exposure as a mole."

Luke whistled softly. "So Weston directed the Dragon Heads

to eliminate you and the photos before you could go back to the cops. Except you escaped with the second roll of film and contacted CIA operative Giles Rehnquist instead."

"Right. And Blake panicked. He orchestrated a hit to silence his own agent in Shanghai. But Rehnquist, immediately noticing he'd picked up a tail, informed another CIA colleague in Washington. He told her he was worried he'd been compromised somehow and he wanted to inform her as insurance. Then when Rehnquist was killed she went straight to the CIA brass and told them his concerns. Once she voiced them on the record, the word was out, and Blake couldn't silence her without raising suspicion."

Luke snorted. "Which meant Weston was *totally* screwed, because now a whole bunch of people knew about you and the photos, plus the fact there was an internal security breach." Luke swore. "The bastard. That's why he contracted the FDS, so he could appear to be handling you objectively while he dealt with his security breach. Meanwhile, he was using *me* to find you so that he could send the Dragon Heads in to finish you off. Christ, that guy is something else."

She smiled, and cupped the side of his face. "Well, he didn't count on you, Luke."

"Nor you, girl." He returned her smile, circling her wrist with his hand. "We make a good team, Jess," he said, drawing her closer to him.

But she held back, a nervousness creeping into her eyes.

He tensed. "What is it, Jess?"

She moistened her lips. "What…are you going to do now, Luke, once you get out of here?"

"We're going to plan a wedding, Jessica, that's what." Concern tightened his features. "You're not thinking of bailing on me now, are you?"

A bolt of emotion shuddered through Jessica and she couldn't stop the sudden flow of crazy tears.

"Jess?"

"I…I thought…" She inhaled shakily, smudging tears across

her face and laughing at the same time. "I…I was just worried you might have forgotten you'd even asked. I…I thought maybe you were just delirious, not thinking…"

He grasped her wrist tight and yanked her down to him. "You want to know something?" His voice was low gravel. Seductive. Strong. "The thought of *you* is what kept me alive, Jessica. You gave me a future to care about, dammit. You made me *want* to live." A ferocious light burned in his gray eyes. "I love you, Jess, and don't you ever forget it."

She bit her lip trying to control her emotion. "I love you, too, Luke," she whispered. "More than you can ever imagine. You're the most solid thing I've ever come across and I am so damn glad you found me that night in Gastown."

He took her face in his strong, rough hands. "Come here."

He kissed her through the salt of her tears, drawing her body close against his, feeling the soft cashmere of her pale pink sweater against his bare arms, the roundness of her breasts against his chest; and Luke knew he'd finally turned the corner. He'd found his way home.

Epilogue

One year later. São Diogo Island.

"You may now kiss the bride," announced the FDS military chaplain to hoots and cheers.

Luke lifted the veil and kissed Jessica under a bower of frangipani blooms in the warm African sun.

In the distance the Atlantic ocean crunched onto sugar-white shores. They were surrounded by those Luke considered family—a close circle of FDS mercenaries, part of the private army of which he was proud to belong.

Jacques Sauvage had invited Luke and Jessica to marry on the island, and Jessica had been delighted to meet the men in Luke's life. Jacques had also flown Jessica's mother over from London for the occasion, as well as Luke's brothers, whom he'd reconnected with after four years.

It was a double celebration, said Jacques, since it was also the fifteen-year anniversary of the Force du Sablé.

Jessica could see that while a military leader at heart, Jacques Sauvage was also a powerfully moral and deeply committed family man—and a tough taskmaster. Luke couldn't have worked with anyone less alpha, she figured. He'd simply crush them with his own stubborn will. And she loved him for it.

As the sky turned deep orange and a chorus of birds heralded the coming twilight, the wedding celebration moved to tables set among giant ficus trees hung with lanterns.

The bride and groom sat at the head table with Jacques and his wife, Olivia, FDS surgeon Hunter McBride and his wife, Sarah, and Sultan Rafiq Zayed with his queen, Dr. Paige Sterling. The three men were the FDS founders and had come together for the anniversary.

Also present was Ubasi ambassador to the United Nations, Jean-Charles Laroque, with his wife, noted psychologist and FDS profiler Dr. Emily Carlin.

The children of several of the couples played barefoot under the trees, laughter ringing out as African musicians began soft xylophone notes and a woman's voice rose in a stirringly passionate rendition of the traditional spiritual song "Sinnerman"—at Luke's request.

Jessica closed her eyes, hijacked by the sheer power of the woman's voice as she sang the words, "Sinnerman, where you gonna run to…" These FDS soldiers had all found a place to run to, she thought, many of them sinnermen themselves in some way. Until they had found brotherhood and purpose again with the FDS.

Luke's brothers were also seated at the main table, alongside Jessica's mother, who was beaming from ear to ear. Jessica smiled warmly at her mom as she fingered the small gold pendant at her neck. Luke had mended it for her after it had been ripped from her throat when the Dragon Heads had abducted her from the Vancouver hotel room. Jessica was proud to wear it for her wedding.

She had a lot to be proud about. She'd fought hard, and won. In partnership with a BBC crew, Jessica had produced a riveting documentary on the rise of the "Red Dragon" and the fall of the CIA chief and his triad wife. She'd reclaimed her profession and she was up for several international news awards.

Luke stood, drawing his bride to her feet at his side. The chatter around the tables fell silent as all eyes turned to them.

Luke raised his glass high. "To the FDS," he said. "To my friend Jacques Sauvage." He turned to his wife. "And to the most beautiful woman in the world, my wife, Jessica Chan." He chinked his glass with Jessica's and looked deep into his bride's hauntingly gorgeous golden eyes, his heart silently busting with overwhelming love and pride.

And joy.

It was a word so easily used, thought Luke, watching her eyes, but a commodity so rarely truly found.

They locked gazes and the world seemed to fade away around them. And Luke knew it was love—her love—that had brought him back to life.

* * * * *

Don't miss
MANHUNTER
The first book in Loreth Anne White's
thrilling new miniseries for
Silhouette Romantic Suspense,
TRUE NORTH
Available November 2008,
wherever Silhouette Books are sold.

Enjoy a sneak preview of
MATCHMAKING WITH A MISSION
by B.J. Daniels,
part of the WHITEHORSE, MONTANA *miniseries.*
Available from Harlequin Intrigue
in April 2008.

Nate Dempsey has returned to Whitehorse to uncover the truth about his past...

Nate sensed someone watching the house and looked out in surprise to see a woman astride a paint horse just on the other side of the fence. He quickly stepped back from the filthy second-floor window, although he doubted she could have seen him. Only a little of the June sun pierced the dirty glass to glow on the dust-coated floor at his feet as he waited a few heart-beats before he looked out again.

The place was so isolated he hadn't expected to see another soul. Like the front yard, the dirt road was waist-high with weeds. When he'd broken the lock on the back door, he'd had to kick aside a pile of rotten leaves that had blown in from last fall.

As he sneaked a look, he saw that she was still there, staring at the house in a way that unnerved him. He shielded his eyes from the glare of the sun off the dirty window and studied her, taking in her head of long blond hair that feathered out in the breeze from under her Western straw hat.

She wore a tan canvas jacket, jeans and boots. But it was the way she sat astride the brown-and-white horse that nudged the memory.

He felt a chill as he realized he'd seen her before. In that very spot. She'd been just a kid then. A kid on a pretty paint horse. Not this one—the markings were different. Anyway, it couldn't have been the same horse, considering the last time he had seen her was more than twenty years ago. That horse would be dead by now.

His mind argued it probably wasn't even the same girl. But he knew better. It was the way she sat the horse, so at home in a saddle and secure in her world on the other side of that fence.

To the boy he'd been, she and her horse had represented freedom, a freedom he'd known he would never have—even after he escaped this house.

Nate saw her shift in the saddle, and for a moment he feared she planned to dismount and come toward the house. With Ellis Harper in his grave, there would be little to keep her away.

To his relief, she reined her horse around and rode back the way she'd come.

As he watched her ride away, he thought about the way she'd stared at the house—today and years ago. While the smartest thing she could do was to stay clear of this house, he had a feeling she'd be back.

Finding out her name should prove easy, since he figured she must live close by. As for her interest in Harper House... He would just have to make sure it didn't become a problem.

* * * * *

Be sure to look for
MATCHMAKING WITH A MISSION
and other suspenseful Harlequin Intrigue stories,
available in April
wherever books are sold.

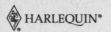

REQUEST YOUR FREE BOOKS!

2 FREE NOVELS PLUS 2 FREE GIFTS!

Silhouette® Romantic

SUSPENSE

Sparked by Danger, Fueled by Passion!

YES! Please send me 2 FREE Silhouette® Romantic Suspense novels and my 2 FREE gifts (gifts are worth about $10). After receiving them, if I don't wish to receive any more books, I can return the shipping statement marked "cancel." If I don't cancel, I will receive 4 brand-new novels every month and be billed just $4.24 per book in the U.S. or $4.99 per book in Canada, plus 25¢ shipping and handling per book plus applicable taxes, if any*. That's a savings of at least 15% off the cover price! I understand that accepting the 2 free books and gifts places me under no obligation to buy anything. I can always return a shipment and cancel at any time. Even if I never buy another book from Silhouette, the two free books and gifts are mine to keep forever.

240 SDN EEX6 340 SDN EEYJ

Name	(PLEASE PRINT)	
Address		Apt. #
City	State/Prov.	Zip/Postal Code

Signature (if under 18, a parent or guardian must sign)

Mail to the **Silhouette Reader Service**:
IN U.S.A.: P.O. Box 1867, Buffalo, NY 14240-1867
IN CANADA: P.O. Box 609, Fort Erie, Ontario L2A 5X3

Not valid to current subscribers of Silhouette Romantic Suspense books.

Want to try two free books from another line?
Call 1-800-873-8635 or visit www.morefreebooks.com.

* Terms and prices subject to change without notice. N.Y. residents add applicable sales tax. Canadian residents will be charged applicable provincial taxes and GST. This offer is limited to one order per household. All orders subject to approval. Credit or debit balances in a customer's account(s) may be offset by any other outstanding balance owed by or to the customer. Please allow 4 to 6 weeks for delivery. Offer available while quantities last.

SRS08

nocturne™

The Bloodrunners
trilogy continues with book #2.

The hunt meant more to Jeremy Burns than dominance—
it meant facing the woman he left behind. Once
Jillian Murphy had belonged to Jeremy, but now she was
the Spirit Walker to the Silvercrest wolves. It would take
more than the rights of nature for Jeremy to renew his
claim on her—and she would not go easily once he had.

LAST WOLF
HUNTING

by RHYANNON BYRD

Available in April wherever books are sold.

Be sure to watch out for the last book,
Last Wolf Watching, available in May.

SN61785

Romantic
SUSPENSE

COMING NEXT MONTH

#1507 DANGER SIGNALS—Kathleen Creighton
The Taken

Detective Wade Callahan is determined to discover the killer in a
string of unsolved murders—without the help of his new partner. Tierney
Doyle is used to being criticized for her supposed psychic abilities, but
even the tough-as-nails—and drop-dead-gorgeous—detective can't deny
what she has uncovered. And Tierney is slowly discovering that working
so closely to Wade could be lethal.

#1508 A HERO TO COUNT ON—Linda Turner
Broken Arrow Ranch

Katherine Wyatt would never trust a man again, until she was forced
to trust the sexy stranger at her family's ranch. Undercover investigator
Hunter Sinclair wasn't looking to get romantically involved, especially
with Katherine. But when she started dating a potential suspect, he had
no choice but to let her in…and risk losing his heart.

#1509 THE DARK SIDE OF NIGHT—Cindy Dees
H.O.T. Watch

Fleeing for his life, secret agent Mitch Perovski is given permission
to use the senator's boat as an out…but he didn't think he'd have the
senator's daughter to accompany him. Kinsey Hollingsworth just wanted
to escape the scandal she was mixed up in. Now she's thrown into a game
of cat and mouse and her only chance for survival is Mitch. Can she
withstand their burning attraction long enough to stay alive?

#1510 LETHAL ATTRACTION—Diana Duncan
Forever in a Day

When Sabrina Matthews is held at gunpoint, the last person she expects
to save her life was SWAT pilot—and ex-crush—Grady O'Rourke.
Grady is shocked when he receives a call informing him his next mission
is to protect Sabrina. Though Grady is confident in his skills, she is the
only woman who can get under his skin. He may be in greater danger of
losing his heart than his life.

SRSCNM0308